C.S. Boag is a former journalist who has also grown potatoes, driven taxis and bulldozers and worked in a hamburger bar. He has travelled many times throughout Australia and to France, speaking enough French not to die there. He was a Sydney City Councillor for six years and holds degrees from NSW and Sydney universities as well as postgraduate qualifications from Macquarie. Besides publishing short stories he has also worked as a columnist for *Woman's Day* and the *Bulletin*. He won the Walter Stone Memorial Prize for Literature in 1986. C.S. Boag lives on a small 'green' holding near Bathurst, NSW, with his wife, Judith. He has five children.

www.csboag.com

By the same author

The Case of the Hood With No Hands

The Case of the Death of a Ladies' Man

C.S. Boag

MISTER RAINBOW

in the Case of the

HORSES FOR CORPSES

XOUM PUBLISHING

Sydney

First published by Xoum in 2013

Xoum Publishing
PO Box Q324, QVB Post Office,
NSW 1230, Australia
www.xoum.com.au

ISBN 978-1-922057-67-9 (digital)
ISBN 978-1-922057-68-6 (print)

Cataloguing-in-publication data is available from the
National Library of Australia

Word count 46,000

Chapter 1

MARKS INCONSISTENT WITH

It's early morning in the city – derelict time – and all around are greasy figures under greasier blankets. They clog Sydney's interstices, the gaps between too much money and mere survival, the crooks and nannies of that bleakest of wastelands between death wish and harsh reality. Wherever you look you'll find them – under concrete overpasses, in hidden corners of parks and shop doorways, behind trees; most of them alive, although you wouldn't always know it.

I'm jogging past Central station when I see the van, and after that – but only because I'm looking – a woman moving silently among the shapeless shapes like an overworked war-zone nurse. She cuts a small figure in old joggers and an even older tracksuit – bending, tending, caressing, assessing, leaving or carrying, before moving on – fluttering over her charges like a heart that won't stop, willing them to survive. As long as I've known her, Annie's cared for lost souls, toiling among the city's destitute, lugging some into her van and carting them to refuges, or taking others to the morgue. Plenty of charities do the same, but Annie's the only one I know does it freelance.

'Hi Annie.'

She straightens and turns. 'Rainbow.' Nice eyes in a nice face, set wide. 'What brings you here?'

'I was on my way to Bondi for an early-morning arm-over when I spotted Gertrude.' Gertrude is Annie's battered splitscreen Kombi. Down the side is written ANNIES VAN in multi-coloured lettering, together with a few too many flowers.

With the toe of my whiteside I nudge a figure slumped in a rose bed. 'They're hopeless cases, you know.'

Annie wipes her face with the back of her hand. 'Someone's got to do something.'

I frown over the figure I just toed. 'Not much doing for this one.'

Annie nods sadly. 'It happens. People bash them. Or they just stop breathing.'

I bend down and pull back the blanket. The clothes are pretty clean. So is the body. 'It's the boot, the brick, the broken bottle – or nothing at all?'

'No shades of grey round here.'

I take a closer look at the body. Odd. 'This wasn't a regular street death. The marks are inconsistent with passing away quietly in the night – or a violent death due to boot, broken bottle or brick.'

'What do you mean?'

'See here. Little cuts, bruises, a few burns. If he wasn't dead, I'd describe this corpse as well-dressed, well-fed and happy.'

Annie looks away. She also looks troubled. 'This isn't the first. There was another one. I don't know what's going on. The weather hasn't been too bad, there hasn't been an epidemic …'

I peer closer. The bloke's young-ish. Nice complexion for a corpse, so not a drinker; fingertips clean, so he didn't smoke himself to death; and no track marks to indicate drugs. 'Look.' I point to his arms. 'And there and there and there again. What could be cigarette burns, but aren't. A couple of bruises, but small ones, not the kind that might have been made by a ham fist, or a length of pipe. Weals to the wrists – and I don't mean cartwheels. A missing fingernail.'

'Exactly like the other one.' I wait for her to go on. She'll go on if there's anything to go on about, and keep quiet if there's not. She's sharp, Annie – nice but sharp – and doesn't miss a trick unless she has to. 'Usually I can help them, Rainbow, but not these ones.'

'The other was male, too?'

She looks at me in surprise. 'Now you mention it – yes.'

'When?'

'Few weeks ago. What are we going to do, Rain?'

'Sorry, but I got enough on my front gate without worrying about this.' Like a swim at Bondi, followed by a date with my daughter, Imogene – the daughter that my ex, Salina, has been threatening to take away. 'The cops'll sort it out.'

Annie shakes her head. 'C'mon, we both know the police won't sort out anything. To them, they're just derelicts. No political strength, no family, no friends. Their wounds are self-inflicted. They're road bumps on the highway to nowhere. Couldn't you –'

'Annie, I care, okay? But right now there are other things I care about more.'

She nods and bends over her next patient, a pink-grey mess in the dull grey dawn, huddled deep in a cavernous declivity of a warped and twisted Moreton Bay fig.

Time to resume my jog. But I'm a long way from the frivolity of Bondi Beach, and this fact is brought into sharp relief when, out of the corner of my eye, I catch sight of something distinctly unmissable – a shapely blonde in leopardskin leotards – dawdling by the bus stop.

Chapter 2

CASINO ROYALE

An hour or so later, I've had my swim – five kilometres up and down Australia's most famous stretch of surf and sand – concentrating on keeping my head underwater for three minutes at a time in order to increase lung power, but also to avoid thinking about Annie and that mysterious corpse. Not to mention the conspicuous blonde in the leopardskin leotards. After all of which I take Imogene on her long-overdue outing to the pictures.

The call comes in on dead-man's mobile No. 3, just as me and the kid are decanting ourselves from the movie house. It's a dame. I don't recognise the voice, only the panic in it.

'We have to save him, Rainbow!' Mostly they give you too much information, but right now there isn't enough to blow your nose on. 'The devils have him in their thrall,' she continues. 'It's as if he can't see left or right as they drag him into the pit. He's not like this at heart. Underneath, he's a decent man, we both know that. It was the – accident.'

Next to me, Imogene's fiddling. In my experience, kids are always fiddling with something – if it's not electronic gimmickry, it's your heart.

'What accident?' I ask.

The panic leaves the voice and is replaced by surprise. 'Surely you remember?' Cultured tones under the surprise, tones that take me smack-bang back in time into the presence of a gorgeous twenty-year-old with a face so beautiful that a joker required shades just to be in its presence. And that memory conjures up another memory – of a soggy afternoon at Royal Randwick and a three-year-old galloper veering out of control across a packed field, with its rider ending up under the hooves of too many horses.

Yeah, I remember all right.

I also remember the jockey that ended up under all those horses.

It's the connection I don't remember.

'Is it always like that, Daddy?' Imogene's eleven, or maybe she's fourteen, and apart from electronic gimmickry, she likes asking questions.

'Hold that thought.' I put my mitt over the cellar-phone and turn my attention to the kid. 'Is what always like what, sweetheart?'

She glances at the punters emerging from the movie house before turning her peepers back to me. 'Is gambling really like *Casino Royale*? Are casinos places of luxury, with beautiful curtains and chandeliers, and aristocratic ladies dressed in silk, and dealers wearing silver armbands and waistcoats with cards on them, and men in tuxedos winning millions, and people driving beautiful cars?'

I tell the kid no, it's not at all like that, before going back to the voice on the phone.

'Rainbow, are you still there?' She doesn't wait for a response. 'They're after him.'

'Who's after whom?'

'The shysters, the racketeers, the hoons – I don't know what you call them – the gambling people, the ones he owes all the money to.' There's the sound of a deep, shuddering breath at the other end of the Telefunken, after which comes the equally unenlightening addendum, 'He can't stop and I didn't know who to turn to. I hope you don't mind, I got your number from your Aunt Rube.'

Rube's the spinster aunt cum private detective who took me in when Dad dumped me after Mum topped herself. Aunt Rube raised me on ballet, old Jimmy Cagney movies, and the principles of detecting.

'So take your friend to gamblers anonymous,' I say.

'I did, but it turned out to be just another opportunity for him to gamble. You know how they sit around listening to each other's stories? Well, Cyril turned it into a – a – I mean, well, he – opened a book on how long the gamblers' resolutions not to gamble would last, and soon everyone was betting on it. In the end, even the facilitator was having a flutter.'

At least I got a name.

'So where is he now, this Cyril of yours?'

'There's someone following us, Daddy.'

I put the voice on hold again while I look at where Imogene's looking. And where Imogene's looking is the following:

1.   Posters featuring giant monkeys, maniacs carrying weapons, and a bunch of beautiful dames trussed wild-eyed to lampposts;

2.   The crumbling pillars of the rerun movie house; and

3.   Only part-hidden behind one of the pillars, that shapely blonde in leopardskin leotards.

Rule numero uno for a tail is never to wear leopardskin leotards.

And rule numero uno for the tail-ee is to work out how come you got a tail.

There's Pandora, the woman in black, the dame that's always there. But this ain't Pandora. There's all the people in all the world who hate me, but something tells me this isn't one of them. And there's the figure I saw when I was checking out the corpses at Central. Coincidence?

I don't do coincidence.

Reason?

There's no reason I can see, unless she just likes the colour of my hat.

Chapter 3

A VOICE FROM THE PAST

'There's always somebody following somebody else, Immo,' I say, slipping into the fatherly reassurance routine. 'It's the way of the world – it's called stalking. And if we can see this particular person, it means she's a rank amateur, and therefore not worth worrying about …'

'What did you say?'

I remember the Telefunken. 'Sorry, I wasn't talking about you.' I nod to Imogene, while readdressing myself to the phone. 'Meanwhile, my question is: where's the pelican now?'

'What?'

'This Cyril character.'

There's a sound like a receiver getting banged against something hard, which tells me either that the dame's in distress, or in a public telephone booth, or both. 'He's busy throwing away what little money we have – not to mention a great deal of money we don't have – trying to win back enough to repay what he's already lost.'

I strain to hear beyond all the emotion – while keeping a weather eye on the dame in the leopardskin leotards only half-hiding her curves behind the pillory.

'We're two months behind in the rent,' the woman goes on. 'He lost our car in a bet with a bloke who came to turn off the gas, over nothing more than a couple of cockroaches that happened to be crossing the sink at the time. And without my knowledge or consent, he pawned a diamond necklace belonging to my great great grandmother – not to mention a pair of priceless Paspaley pearl earrings I'd kept from my modelling days. Meanwhile, we haven't had a decent feed for months. He –'

'Look, I'm really sorry, lady, but I gotta go.'

'Rainbow, if I don't get Cyril back now, he'll be lost forever.'

The trouble with life is it's got history in it. And part of my history contains a dame that once upon a time rescued me from the depredations of a busted marriage and the equally unfriendly floor of a speakeasy. I take a deep breath. 'Okay, okay. So where is this –?'

The kid answers the question meant for the dame. 'She's still behind that post over there, watching us.'

'Sorry, Immo, I was talking to the dame. And not that one – the one on the phone.' I aim my dulcets back into the dulcimer. 'Sorry, I missed the last bit – where is he?'

'He's at the betting joint.'

'Which particular betting joint would that be?'

'The one that spells R-A-T-S backwards. Please, Rainbow, can't you rescue him – if only for old times' sake?'

Old times have a lot to answer for. 'Look, lady –'

'Will you stop calling me *lady*. My name's Angela Golightly.'

The Angel that was. My angel of mercy. The dame that took me in and got me back up to speed, after which we did the mutual-parting trick, and after a suitable interval Angel took up with her jockey, after which –

'Yeah, well, look, I got my daughter with me, see, and –'

'Oh, yes, I remember. *Imagine*, wasn't it? She was a real sweetie.'

Imagine must have been how Angela saw the kid at the time, the kid she would have preferred not to exist.

'Im-*oh*-gene.'

'Oh, of course – Im-oh-gene.'

There's too much information going back and forth for comfort – but I'll replace the dead-man's mobile with another one, courtesy of my little mate Rory. And after that, no-one will be able to tie me to the Angel dame, or her to me, or the kid to either of us, and I'll be home – or what passes for home these days – free. Me and Angela Golightly will be nothing more than ships that once-upon-a-turbulent-sea, happened to pass in the night.

'Do give her my love, Rainbow.'

'Yeah, I'll do that.'

'What would the little darling have been then? Three? Six? Your Imagine must be quite the grown-up now. Which means you could take her to the casino, couldn't you? The whole thing would only take a minute. Then you and Imagine could both go back to doing whatever it was you were doing before I so rudely interrupted.'

'I'm not taking my daughter to a casino.'

'Please? For me?'

I glance at the kid who's playing with whatever she's playing with. 'I –'

'It'll only take a moment.'

What's a moment, compared to a lifetime? I take another deep breath. 'Okay, Angel, I'll get your husband back for you.' I adjust to work mode. 'What's he look like now?' Once he was a handsome pocket jockey, but then there was the accident.

'He looks like too many horses ran over him.' It's a clever reply, but she must figure she owes me more than a clever reply, because she adds, 'Aside from which, he'll be with Lord Haw-Haw.'

I rack the grey matter. 'This Lord Haw-Haw joker – he a gambler, too?'

This brings a laugh from the other end, and the laughter's sad enough to tear my heart out. 'Oh, Rainbow, Lord Haw-Haw's not a person, it's a – a horse.'

I frown. 'What do you mean, a *horse*?'

Chapter 4

ABANDON HATS, ALL YOUSE THAT ENTER HERE

There's a pause while Angel reins in the chuckle. 'Just what I said – Lord Haw-Haw's a horse.'

I struggle to come to terms with what she's telling me.

'Not a *real* horse – just one of those cuddly toys that people give babies. We bought it when we were trying to – when we hoped we might … But then there was the accident and Cyril's legs were so badly hurt he could never ride again. Also he couldn't, you know – I mean, well, we were never going to have a family after the accident. So instead of being for the baby, Lord Haw-Haw became *Cyril's* cuddly toy.'

Two beats of silence, then, 'It doesn't *mean* anything, but Cyril took to carrying Lord Haw-Haw with him wherever he went. It was sort of – company for him. And he insists that he brings him luck.' Another mirthless attempt at a laugh from the other end. 'That's what he *says*. Which is all very well, except that Cyril and luck have become, well, estranged. Only it's more than that, a lot more. You see, Cyril's a – well, a depressive. Blame the accident, blame his misfortune since then, blame me – but somehow Haw-Haw seems to – well, buck him up when he's down. It's as if he *needs* that thing with him to – survive. Does that make sense to you?'

I do another deep breath, the one with the three-minute underwater survival potential in it. 'As much sense as anything does in this world, Angel.'

After I click off, I check out the figure failing to hide its curves behind the faux pilaster in the foyer. She's of medium height, and with no standout characteristics apart from the obvious. So – except for the leopardskin leotards that tend to distract attention towards instead of away from her – she'd answer to the description of the perfect follower.

The kid glances up from her gizmo. 'Are we going home now, Daddy?'

Home is an old tub parked in Sydney Harbour, a once-upon-a-time ferry with a smashed-in bow and a wraparound pedestrian mall. I call her the *Wooden No* – as in *Where do you live? Wooden No.* But that's not what Immo's talking about. Her home's where the mother, Salina, is, the narrow-gutted scrap of real estate on Castanet Close where we used to play happy families – before I realised I was playing to an empty house, and a memory.

'We got a detour to make first, sweetheart.'

The kid nods. 'Mummy says your whole life is nothing more than a series of detours.'

I'm careful not to reply with anything that might be considered defamatory. 'People could say that of anyone, kid.'

Imogene suddenly goes thoughtful. 'Mummy's going through one of those detours now. She met a man she calls Mr Perfect – although she says that after you anyone would seem perfect. I haven't met him yet, but she says he's got a lot of money, which is another – But don't worry, Daddy, I'm keeping tabs on him.'

I glance down at her. 'How are you doing that?'

She waves the gizmo at me. 'Like this.' She flicks a switch.

'Yeah.' My voice emerges out of the technology. *'Well, look, I got my daughter with me, see, and –'*

Pause.

'Im-oh-gene.'

Longer pause, long enough for me to see where this is going.

'Yeah, sure.'

Another pause.

'I'm not taking my daughter to a casino.'

Pause.

'I –'

Pause.

'Okay, Angel, I'll get your husband back for you …'

The kid switches her recorder off, and a look like a purring cat takes over her dial-up. 'Like you always say, Daddy, a person's gotta do what a person's gotta do.' She shakes her head as she files the recording studio in a poche in her jeans. 'And you just promised someone that you'd take me to a casino, so you can't get out of it. I've got you on record.' She shakes her fourteen- or is it forty-year-old head. 'After *Casino Royale*, I want to see the real thing. All that glamour and sophistication.' I go pale. 'Oh, don't worry, I won't tell Mummy. Plus I can keep an eye on that woman who's following us.'

I glance around. The old crowd of movie goers has been replaced by a new crowd of movie goers, but there's no sign of the dame not well enough hidden behind a pillar, fake or otherwise. 'What woman?'

But the kid's moved on, too. She's been to the movie and now she wants to experience the reality. She tugs at my jacket. It's still got sand in the pockets from the swim at Bondi. 'Come on, Daddy, stop jumping at shadows and take your daughter to the casino.'

In Sydney town, it's not what you know, but how much money you got when you know it. It's a way of thinking that grows no cherries, in my opinion, but it's still the raison d'être of most of the inhabitants of this burg. Everyone wants a slice of bacon and most punters believe that places like the casino are where it's served. Wrong. The casino's where people go to get poor, the place where punters part company with whatever they had to begin with, and go into hock for the rest.

There's a lot of pathways to gambling and there are plenty of entrances to the Star. I take the mechanical steps, followed by the black-and-gold stairway to Hell, and the kid follows. Too much fake marble, too many fake flowers, too much false hope, and too much security.

'Where do you think you're going?' He's wearing

a purple tie with a couple of dice doing the tango on it, he's waving a wand like the Fairy Godmother on steroids, and he must be hard of hearing because there's a curly black wire sprouting out of one of his ears.

'We're about to enter your establishment.'

'Not wearing that hat you're not.'

'Why, don't you like the colour?'

'The colour's fine, pal, it's the hat I don't like – not to mention the insect life under it.' The goon waves his weapon sniffer at the wall beside him. 'Like the sign says, for people that can read, we got dress rules, and those rules say that your headwear's illegal.' He then produces a cackle as spontaneous as the 700-year-old misquote he's about to hand me. 'So, in the words of the bard: *Abandon hats, all youse that enter here.*'

Never trust jokers that misquote Dante. 'The Devil can cite scripture for his purpose,' I snarl.

The goon frowns. 'What did you just say?'

Chapter 5

CASINO NORMALE

'I'm just trying to maintain the status quote.' I chuck the hat down the golden stairway and it fetches up on a fake aspidistra. 'Satisfied now?'

But the goon's wagging his head as well as his metal detector, at the same time as he's talking to his tie, the purple one with the matching pair of dice on it. 'Yeah, Joe? Look, I got a danger man here. Yeah, you got the cameras on him? The one with the orange-check promissory note, the two-tone footwear, and the kid.' He nods at the tie without taking his eyes off the object in question, me. 'Gotcha.' He hangs up his tie, and waves me back to oblivion. 'You can't come in, anyway, on account of the age limit.'

'Since when was there a limit on age?'

'Since the Devil invented gambling.'

I'm Mr Anonymous. Which means I haven't got a driver's licence, a credit card, or a permit for the gun that I left on the boat in order to be with the kid. Accordingly, I haven't got proof of anything, even if I wanted to prove it.

'Look, pal,' I say, 'use your ee-whys, if not your brain. I'm forty-something. How can that be the wrong age to lose money?'

He sets his feet apart on the fake marble floor, while his knuckles whiten on the wand. 'I'm not talking about you, wise guy.' He waves his wand at Imogene. 'I'm talking about the kid. If she's under eighteen – and my guess is she's way under – then she can't come in.'

I don't know how old Imogene is, but I'm pretty sure she's not eighteen yet. It doesn't stop me arguing the toss, or the tosser – take your pick. 'Afraid she'll take your money?'

'No, I'm afraid she can't come in, period.'

'So what am I supposed to do with her? Check her into the cloak room?'

That's when the goon turns into something he wasn't five minutes ago. 'No, you can try being a proper father, and keep her away from places of evil.'

The kid's busy excavating the fedora from the faux greenery when I return.

'The man up there says we gotta go,' I say.

When she straightens, she's frowning. 'But, Daddy, you promised you'd get that lady's husband back for her.'

I shrug the jacket that hasn't got a gat in it. 'So now I can't.'

'But you promised.'

'Some promises just can't be kept, Immo.'

'That's not what you always tell me.' She gestures around. 'Besides, I'm safe here.'

I quarter the environs. A bunch of fancy stores, the aforementioned fake flowers, too many punters arriving to donut too much dough-re-you to the richest men in Australia, and a couple of garbage bins at the foot of the stairs. I remember Little

Orphan Annie and the corpse at Central station.

'Sweetheart, this is Sydney, which means you're not safe anywhere.'

Imogene gets that look, the one that says I'm messing with forces I don't understand. 'Daddy, thanks to you, I know how to look after myself. Anyway, it's broad daylight and this is a public thoroughfare. And you won't be long – you're just going in to rescue that lady's husband.' She holds up the recorder. 'Besides, while I'm waiting, I can practise being a detective.'

I think a lot of things, but mostly I think of what my ex-wife Salina would say if she found out I'd abandoned her daughter at the Gates of Hell – and weigh that against a debt I've got to a memory. 'Look, I'm sorry, Immo, but I can't.'

The kid's planted her feet firmly on the ground, like she's pretty certain I can. 'You've got to let me go. If you don't, I'll end up being dependent on you forever.'

I take a deep breath racked with uncertainty. 'Well, if you're sure …'

Imogene takes hold of my sleeve with the hand that hasn't got the hat in it. 'Sure I'm sure. If you keep me wrapped up in cotton wool I'll never become what I *want* to become. How can I become a real-life detective if you … I'll just wait on the bottom step until you come out, all right? And don't worry, I'll be as safe as – as the *Wooden No*.'

As an analogy it could have done with a bit of fine-tuning. But I hand over my blade and shrug myself out of the jacket and turn it inside out, so it's no longer orange any more but black. I then make my way up yet another staircase that leads to the gambling parlour. At the top, I pause, turn and look down. The knife's no longer visible and Immo's gripping the gizmo she records people with, along with my hat, and she must have sensed me looking because she glances up. She seems a lot smaller than I'd like her to be, but I tell myself it's just the perspective. I give her the thumbs-up and she juggles the recorder into the hat and gives me the thumbs-up back – together with that reassuring smile of hers.

So. I've altered my profile. No hat, different-coloured coat and, above all, no kid. Also I'm facing a different Cerberus with a wired-up lug hole. No doubt he's been told to watch out for a weirdo, but I'm a different kind of weirdo to the one he's been told to watch out for, so he waves me through.

If you've seen one of these joints, whether it's Monaco, Nevada, Atlantic City, Baden-Baden, or Hobart – the things spawn like maggots on a dead dog – you've seen them all. The aim is to relieve punters of their livelihood, while giving back less than nothing in return.

Music plays and security pretends not to be security, while down-at-heel derros and round-shouldered crones perch on flick-back stools in front of rows of poke-your-heart-outs bearing monikers like Crazy Harry, Blonde with a Wand and Yours for the Asking. There were no pokies in

Casino Royale, but *Casino Royale* this ain't. This is the real world. And what counts in the real world is not how things look or feel, but what brings in the most cash to the big boys. And what brings in the readies in these places is the extra oxygen they put in the air-conditioning to make people feel more like gambling; the absence of clocks and windows to remove unnecessary distractions; while the constant clink of bottles against glasses says they got the all important alcohol angle covered as well. There's definitely no pearls and no evening dresses. At the Rats, you got gambling stripped to its barest inessentials. There's only one winner, and that's the jokers running it.

I check out the CCTV cameras as I pass a geezer urging on a Big Six – Money Wheel, Wheel of Fortune, call it what you will. With an eighty-to-one chance of a payout it's the biggest rip off since the postage stamp.

Chapter 6

DOWN AMONG THE GAMBLERS

'Looking for something, big boy?' She's got cherry-red lips, a drinks tray, and cleavage like the bum crack on an overweight labourer.

I hunch the shoulders. 'Yeah, I'm looking for a friend.'

She leans forward. Probably should have checked the frock was shrink-proof before she wore it. 'Aren't we all?'

'Not that kind of friend. I'm looking for a gimp with a limp.'

She throws her weight on one hip, which does interesting things to her cleavage, and the drinks tray looks like it's only kept level with gimbals. 'I can do limp.'

At a nearby table a bloke of Middle Eastern appearance is being taken to the cleaners, the House dealing him a pair of jokers only lightly disguised as drink waiters. The muscle's barely apparent as he's shuffled away to the little room under the stairs, where the House turns public embarrassments private.

'It's not the limp I'm after,' I tell the dame, 'but the guy wearing it.'

'Oh, so you're one of *those*.'

'I'm not one of anything, lady, unless it's one of a kind.'

The fake marble floor under my whitesides is unforgiving, and so is the look the dame shoots me as the music they dish out along with the extra oxygen segues into *Ain't She Sweet*. At the next table, a geezer in a wheelchair gets dealt another losing hand, and the Guardian behind the croupier behind the cards checks his little screen to ensure the House is raking off as much as it can, without breaking any obscenity laws.

I'm minding my own business, busy counting CCTV cameras – twenty-three or thereabouts – when a weightlifter appears by my side.

'Can I help you, sir?'

I keep the arms loose and hanging forward – a la James Cagney in *Public Enemy*, plus every other movie he ever appeared in – ready for anything that might come my way. 'What's with this joint? All of a sudden everyone wants to help me.'

The weightlifter is wearing a suit, but that's not enough to make him civilised. 'It's just that I don't see you gambling, sir.'

'I don't see *you* down among the hard balls, either.'

He tenses. 'I'm not paid to gamble, as I only bet on certainties. And for my money, it's a certainty that you spell trouble.'

I got a job to do, and it doesn't include offloading thugs into poker machines. Not only that, Imogene's waiting outside. 'Sorry, pal, I'm looking for the McDonald's.'

'The what?'

'You know, the place where they take your hard-earned, smile too much, and ask if you want chips with that.'

The weightlifter's ready to let fly. 'Just like I thought, a wise guy.'

'But not wise enough not to lose, buster.' I start towards the money cage, slow enough not to trigger any alarm bells in the bloke's head, but fast enough not to give him time to work out what I just told him.

Steaming's when a punter chucks everything he's got into the ring to make good his losses. That's exactly what Cyril Golightly's up to when I finally locate him. He's in the company of a bunch of other shills and is hunched over a scratch pile of poker chips clutching a moth-eaten beast of a blue-and-white toy horse. It's awful – a crazy-eyed, leering-toothed and balding thing about the size and build of an overweight chihuahua.

'Would you care to join us, sir?' asks the dealer.

The chair next to Cyril looks lonely, so I roll it out and keep it company. Once he was an acquaintance but now he's a gambler, with eyes for nothing but the mirage of the big win. He's slouched in his low roller's seat, head barely visible above the table, hugging his ugly furball and looking at his cards like a kid peeking at something he shouldn't through a walk-up-and-bend-down keyhole.

I check out my cartes-de-sejour while I consider

my next move. Imogene's outside and she can't stay outside forever, security's circling, and I got to work out a way of removing Cyril without overexciting the gendarmes.

'Are you playing, sir?' the dealer asks again. 'Or are you just here for the ambience?'

It comes out *ambulance*. I dribble out a couple of McDonald's chips while cocking an eyebrow at Cyril. The music keeps playing and the oxygen keeps pumping and the one-armed bandits keep doing their ding-a-ling thing, and the dealer continues to lead the card players by the nose on their roundabout to nowhere.

I talk out of the side of my moosh. 'I'm getting you out of here, Cyril.'

I receive a glance from the ex-hoop, but it's like a grimace from his pony – a look with no recognition in it: two greasy eyeballs in a pair of streaky bowls of soup, lips as tight as a millionaire's wallet, and an expression on his phyzog that says he reckons he could be another James Bond, and that it matters.

'I know nothing but the value of my cards and of silence, mate, so leave me alone.'

I shake the noggin. 'Come on, mate, don't you remember me? I'm –'

The automated voice interposes. 'Are you playing, sir? Or perhaps you'd like to start a sewing circle.'

After half-a-dozen hands, my pile of tiddly-winks has halved. The shuffle machine continues to deal out more hope slips, and a sign on the green-baize table says we can attempt to control our barely-controllable urge to gamble by contacting a nice person on the following number.

'Look, Cyril …' But I'm talking to the toy horse.

'Excuse me.' He turns to the muscle behind the dealer, otherwise known as the Ladderman. 'This person's disrupting my play, and I find myself wondering if he's a stooge of the management.'

The Ladderman exchanges glances with the pit boss, following which he moves around the table. 'I'm sorry, sir, but we thought he was a friend of yours.'

Cyril shakes his head. 'I wouldn't know him from Saddam.'

The pit boss leans over my shoulder. 'In that case, I'm afraid I'm going to have to ask you to leave. Or change seats. Or perhaps tables. Nothing personal, but Mr Golightly objects to your being here.'

I firm up my prospects. 'I'd prefer to stay where I am.'

Phase one.

The muscle leans so close that I can smell his eau-de-colon. 'And we'd prefer that you didn't.' I sense the fist tighten on my rollie chair. 'So if you don't mind …'

'But I do.'

Phase two.

The grip tightens. 'Then I'm going to have to ask you to leave.'

'You and whose army?'

Which moves us nicely and naturally into phase three.

Chapter 7

THE DEAD MAN'S HAND

Aunt Rube always said that if there was a God, She'd only help those who help themselves. But no-one's helping Cyril, so it looks like it's up to me.

I straighten suddenly so that my parietal bone comes into contact with the ape's mandible. At the same time, I slap the wheelie chair into reverse, simultaneously slamming my foot against the bar of the table so the back of the chair rams into the thug's fruit and vegetables, reducing him to a very active part of the pattern on the Axminster, after which I grab hold of Cyril and his donkey.

'Okay, high roller, I'm taking you from your palace of dreams.'

No-one's looking our way, if you don't count the twenty-three CCTV cameras, a thousand and one gamblers, twenty meetya maids, and security. Meanwhile, Dean Martin's crooning *White Christmas* over the Tannoy.

With his free mitt Cyril's clutching anything he can get his hands on. 'No, you're not!' He tightens his grip on the chair and the horse. 'I'm staying where I am!'

When jockeys come into the straight, they get themselves high up out of the saddle and lean forward into fresh air. That's just what Cyril does when I yank the pew out from under him – leaning well forward with his bum out, feet twisted around the chrome-plated foot rails of his chair like they're stirrups, while clinging onto the cream-coloured lip of the green baize like it's reins. The only difference is, his horse is in his armpit instead of under him.

'Don't be Cyril, stupid!'

The cavalry moves in. Jokers that were posing as drink waiters and dames that were pretending to be dames suddenly reveal themselves to be neither. Cyril's collar comes off, and when his cards scatter I see that they're bulls and eights – otherwise known as the dead man's hand, because legend has it some poor bastard went down in a hail of bullets holding it. But Cyril's not going to die. Not right now. Not if I can help it.

'Come on, mate, if only for Angela's sake.'

'Who's Angela?'

The horse finds its way into Cyril's other armpit, and his shirt buttons mix it with the chips, while his feet and fists lock harder onto the table's protuberances.

Something's got to give, and it's the table.

An alarm bell starts ringing. Cyril's got the horse tucked under his arm, and I've got Cyril tucked under mine, as I get the three of us onto the next available table, from where it's only a short hop onto a poker machine, at which point we're nicely within reach of a low-flying chandelier.

Gamblers' ultimate aim is to beat the system that's beating them and suddenly it looks like they got the chance to do just that. A couple of security turn into birds and go flying. Poker faces take to the carpet. Chips find their way into punters' pockets. I take to the air and take Cyril and his piebald mate with me. The chandelier carries us to the next bank of pokies. A sign warns anyone that cares to read it that in case of malfunction the management regrets that there'll be no payouts. We land on Sweet Queen and the machine malfunctions. It pays out. Never trust the signs in a casino. Heavies appear on the walkway and on the double but there's not much they can do. I convey Cyril on a falling fruit machine to ground zero, get him into a fireman's bend, and head for the departure lounge.

By this stage the joint's in automatic lockdown, but the main entrance features no more than a real security guard and another fake bunch of flowers. I offload Cyril into the flowers, take out the security guard, and after that it's slippy-slide time down the moving staircase to freedom …

… but no Imogene. Where the blazes has she got to?

Cyril is struggling. 'I got to get back to the table!'

I clout him over the head and he quietens down. Now I have to lug him as well as the toy horse, but at least he's no longer struggling. I resume my search for the kid. This is where I left her, at the bottom of the stairs, minding my hat and her recorder, as well as her own business. Only she isn't here now.

Possibility numero uno: She left of her own accord. A possibility not even worth considering. Imogene's too smart for that.

Possibility numero duo: A cop, playing it by the book, asks the kid, Where's yer father? At which point Imogene screams the kind of scream that only she can scream, because I've taught her to take shameless advantage of people who play it by the book. Only I didn't hear any screams, which means it probably wasn't a cop. Which is a bastard, because I can do cops.

Possibility numero trio: She's been abducted by a person or persons unknown.

Chapter 8

HELL HATH NO FURY

There's no time for entertaining – possibilities or otherwise – because sure enough a cop's coming our way. He's got lots of equipage hanging off him – yellow stun-gun, head banger, handcuffs, Glock – even though he's barely out of nappies. I toss him a reassuring smile and receive a reassuring smile in return, albeit laced with uncertainty. I backload Cyril and make for the rubbish bin by the escalators. I peer inside. Half a McDonald's quarter-pounder. Two empty cigarette packs. My red fedora with something grey and metallic nestling inside it.

'Excuse me, sir.' Of course the cop's playing it by the book.

I do the same and nod at Cyril. 'He's had one too many, officer.'

The cop considers his options and can't find any. 'Oh. Well, good luck with that.'

The horse is under one arm and Cyril's over the other while I reach down into the bin and grab my fedora and what's in it. I then heft Cyril and his toy horse into safer keeping, put the whitesides into gallop mode, and head for the hills.

Normally, I'd deliver my charge to his place of residence, but this isn't normally, because Immo's still missing. So I offload Cyril, shut him the hell up again, grab the recorder out of the hat, slap it into reverse, press STOP, and after that, PLAY.

The gizmo produces a familiar voice. '*… there are around eleven persons of Middle Eastern appearance going up the centre staircase. Dead ahead, a goon, 190 centimetres, beefy, grey suit. To the right, a kid nagging his mum. Further south, two women, then a cop. Women and cop speak. I sense a camaraderie here. What's that all about? Sorry, Daddy, that's conjecture. Cop leaves. Women looking my way. I hand them a smile, the one that says I haven't been dumped outside a casino by my uncaring father — that's a joke, Daddy — but am here of my own accord. Looks like they'll leave me alone …*'

Cyril moves. I switch off the machine, clout him again, then switch it back on.

'*Correction. Women returning. Description: first, what you'd describe as beautiful. Blue eyes. Just your type, Daddy. Second: middle-aged, bit frumpy, brown hair, and the kind of eyes you don't mess with …*'

This is followed by a voice a couple of paces away that's not playful — and not Imogene's. '*Where's your father then, darling? Playing the pokies, is he?*' Scrabbling sounds. '*Come on, you can tell your Aunt Phoebe.*'

I hear the kid muttering she can do anything but.

Then the same voice again. '*So where do you live, darling?*'

After which, Imogene's voice returns. '*Aunt Phoebe what?*'

No opportunity wasted. Immo's angling for a name while the dame's still in unsuspecting mode.

'*Why, Aunt Phoebe Riesling, darling.*'

The kid, sotto voce, '*The Riesling woman's grabbing for my hand, the one without the hat and recorder in it.*' Sound of struggle, of shoe soles scuffling for a foothold. '*Could you leave me alone, please? I promise I'm all right.*'

Another voice, also female, only firmer this time, more decisive. '*And I can promise you that you're not.*'

We've taken a cab and reach the boulevard around the corner from Salina's place in Castanet Close. Cyril – aka the root cause of all my problems – is leaning against me cuddling his pony. My ex is home. I pretend nothing untoward's happened, and hand her the recorder.

'Can you return that to Imogene for me, Sal?'

She looks down at the gizmo like it's a scorpion. 'Jesus, Rainbow.'

'I take it she's here. In case you didn't realise, I arranged with Imogene to make her own way home, in order to teach her self-reliance.'

'Bullshit!' Sal's eyes flash, her nostrils flare like a lollied-up thoroughbred's, and she waves my knife about in my face like it's got blood on it. 'Can you believe I found Imogene with this? That was after a couple of women brought her home, telling me it was my duty to stop my husband gambling. My husband! My duty! Do you have any idea how I felt when they said that?'

I don't want to know how she felt when they said anything, but I can't tell Salina that. Apart from which, she's going to tell me anyway.

'I felt an anger towards you greater than any I have ever felt before. In fact, I wanted to kill you. I felt as low as a worm. Here were these two women lecturing me on the duties of motherhood and what made it worse was they were right.' Gasp of indrawn breath like she's coming up from the depths of a very deep sea. 'It's hard to believe I married you, Rainbow, and then had a kid by you. The horrible thing is that unmarrying you didn't do anything to correct an almost unbearable situation.'

'Look, Sal, it won't happen again. The situation was beyond my control. I –'

Sal shakes her head. Hell hath no fury like a woman shaking her head. 'You're dead right it won't happen again.' She takes in the mess of humanity hugging its toy horse by my side, and just as quickly takes it out again. 'And do you know why, Rain-bloody-bow? Because I'm taking my daughter away, that's why. And do you want to know something else? You couldn't stop me if you tried. And you couldn't stop me for the very simple reason that you don't exist.' There's a lot of hand waving. 'Non-persons can't take people to court, non-persons can't have people arrested, non-persons have no recourse to the law, non-persons –'

'Look, Sal –'

'No, you look, Rainbow. And when you do, you'll see a future without your daughter in it.'

'Well, that was a success.'

I'd clout Cyril over the head again but that would only temporarily alleviate my feelings, as well as rendering him senseless, meaning I'd have to lug him and his stupid horse home to his missus.

I sigh. 'What's with the toy, anyway, mate?'

He hugs the thing closer, as if fearful I might try to yank it off him. 'It brings me luck.'

'If it's bringing you luck, you'd be in a bloody bad way without it.'

Chapter 9

ANGEL

She was the kinda dame that stopped traffic just by sashaying down the boulevard. A mannequin? Give me a break. Mannequins wear clothes. In Angel's case, the clothes wore her. She soared on golden wings in an Olympian stratosphere, far above anything they cared to garb her in – be it Giotto, Givenchy or Gutter. She was a ballet, a song, a poem, a dream.

It wasn't just that she was beautiful – any dame can be beautiful. No, Angel was like her name says. And that's what she was to me, an angel that put the word 'hope' back in my lexicon. Through a blood-red haze from the floor of the speakeasy, this vision took something off and mopped my face with it.

After which she took me home, where she took off some more.

At the time, home for Angela Pendlebury-Hart was the kind of apartment you read about in dime novels. She was a classy model, and as a result she lived in a classy abode. Her pad took up the entire top rung of the highest piece of real estate in Sydney, and possessed the kind of view most jokers only have courtesy of Google Earth. I get vertigo just thinking about it. Angel was a high flier, while I didn't have a head for heights. But ours was one of those affairs that – while it was never going to have staying power – lasts a lifetime. We were still mates after we split. Even after she hooked up with Cyril, at the time a jockey worth putting the farm on. Even after she married him. Even after my own horse and carriage crashed and I went to live on the *Wooden No*, while Angela Golightly – née Pendlebury-Hart – continued on her heady journey through the stratosphere.

Or so I thought.

I'm sure as hell thinking it no longer as Wobblefoot, with Lord Haw-Haw leering under his arm, reins up at a hole in the wall bearing a sign some wag has doctored to read 'TOiLET'. It's one of a ragged string of bulldoze jobs in inner-west Camperdown adjoining the murder and mayhem of Parramatta Road.

'Hi Rainbow.'

If it wasn't for the voice – plus the faint glimmer of the bangle that's hanging from the micro-thin wrist – I'd say it wasn't the same dame, while in the dim light of the decrepit tenement I'm willing myself to think otherwise. But it's not enough to be willing. The joint's horrible, the smell is worse, and the woman crumpled against the paint-peeling wall bears as much resemblance to the beauty I once knew as a wireframe dressmaker's dummy to a flesh-and-blood model. Gone is the fluidity, the sex appeal and the looks. In its place is a haggard scarecrow garbed in rags, thin as a mass murderer's alibi, and with eyes as sunken as her hopes. If it wasn't for the voice … It's the voice on the phone, the one that rang when me and Imogene were leaving the movie house, the kind of voice you want to close your eyes and drift off to sleep on.

'Hi Rainbow,' she says again, like she's afraid I mightn't have heard her the first time.

I shake my thoughts out of a beautiful past and back to a bleak reality. 'Hi – Ange.' That's when I drop the glossy-white lie. White lies are cheap – something like my feelings right now towards her husband. 'You haven't changed a bit.'

She aims for a smile, misses bad, and comes up with a tragedienne's grimace, at the same time brushing a cobweb of hair out of one eye with a hand as substantial as a whisper. 'You never were a good liar.' She turns away. 'But thanks for rescuing Cyril.'

The useless bastard perched beside her is as lopsided as Angel's grin. He's gripping onto his stupid horse with one hand and scratching his backside with the other, while the traffic thunders by outside like malevolent Destiny.

I make a lunge for the bright side of this scenario, and come up with the jewellery. 'I see you still got the blingle-bangle.'

She grimaces again. 'Rainbow, believe me, I'd die before I'd part with it.' When she raises her coathanger arm, a stray patch of light catches the bauble. 'Whenever I'm in danger of forgetting who I am – or rather, who I used to be – I look at this bangle. I find it somehow – comforting.'

I want to say something but there's nothing to say. I want to stay, but I can only take so much. 'Well, nice to see you again, Ange.' I glance at Cyril and his toy horse. I ought to say what you say at such times – *Look after her* – but the words stick in my throat. Instead, I return my attention to his victim. 'I'll always be there for you, chickadee.' After that, I turn and head for what passes for a door in this joint. I've paid my dues to the past. Now it's time to do something about the present.

But the beautiful voice stops me. 'Do you mean that, Rainbow?'

I pause. My knuckles whiten on the door handle. 'Do I mean what?'

'That you'll always be there for me.'

I take a deep breath. It's got the scent of mould and of something rotten in it, as well as more than a hint of a shared past. But I'm still inside the hovel, looking at the door, like just looking might get me out of here. 'Of course I mean it.' Only right now I'm wishing I didn't, because I know what's coming next.

'Then would you save Cyril for me?'

I stay where I am. 'I just saved Cyril for you.'

'I don't mean just now, I mean from gambling. From – himself.'

When I let go of the door handle, it's like I'm letting go of Imogene. And when I turn around, it's like I'm saying that the letting-go might be permanent. In the gloom, Angel is gripping the spare mitt of the useless husband who's clutching the toy horse, like a drowning woman clutching the waterlogged flotsam of a boat that sank to the bottom of the ocean of life long ago.

My mouth goes dry. 'Do you want to spell that out for me, Ange?'

Chapter 10

RIDING FOR A FALL

So she spells it out for me. 'Cyril and I – well, as you know, we were both pretty successful in our own right. I was doing well with the modelling, while Cyril was a top jockey, riding for the best stables, and winning every race that mattered. So, separately, we enjoyed a great deal of *material* success.'

Now for the *immaterial* success.

'But we both knew there was more to life than money. And when we met, we recognised something in each other.' She looks down at Cyril and clearly sees something I can't. 'And that was that we – we were both somehow different from all that. We –'

'Ange, you lost me when you started using words of more than one syllable.' Every moment here is a lifetime away from my daughter. 'Why don't you get to the point?'

She takes a deep breath. Once, that breath would have set me quivering, but now it's not much more than a harsh wind in a bleak field.

'Most A-Listers have a level of social awareness that goes no deeper than their bank accounts. When Cyril and I met, we weren't like that. So we got together, and shortly after that, we got married – well, you know all that, Rainbow: after all, you came to the wedding.'

I nod. I was there when the preacher asked if anyone present saw cause why Cyril and Angel shouldn't get hitched, and said nothing.

'But then Cyril had the accident and then, of course, the big payout. And so I abandoned my career to look after him.'

There's still time. I can still crawl out of this warren of no return and set about trying to claw back my daughter. But instead all I do is murmur, 'Still, with all that love floating around, if you were in some sort of race to happiness, the bookies would have had you as odds-on favourites to be first over the line.'

Angel shakes her head. 'The favourites don't always take home the marbles, Rainbow, you know that. Besides which, after the accident, our race seemed to be fixed. Cyril's legs were ruined, which meant he could never race again. He had the big payout, but he also had a lot of time on his hands. And, of course, he wanted to look after me. So ...'

There's more – much more. I can see that by the way the three of them – the dame, the ex-jockey, and his toy horse – are propping each other up.

'So Cyril took to gambling. In the beginning, he won. He knew jockeys, he knew horses and he knew form. Above all, he knew the system. But then the horses stopped running true to the system and he began losing – badly. He branched out and lost even more badly. He owed people money. Then there was Cameron.'

I turn and take the fateful step back into the gloom. 'Cameron?'

Cyril disentangles himself from his missus and, still hugging his evil-looking toy, limps away.

Suddenly, Angel doesn't know what to do with her hands. 'Cameron's –' She waves the hands she doesn't know what to do with at the threadbare carpet, the crappy sink, and a future that's there in name only. 'Sorry, I'm being neglectful. Can I get you a – a …'

Cyril breaks in. 'If you're going to suggest a cup of tea, we haven't got any – cups *or* tea.'

'… a glass of something, then.'

'There's no something, either.'

'What about water?'

'Don't you remember? They turned off the water – along with the gas.'

Angel manages a rueful smile. 'Then at least we won't be able to kill ourselves by sticking our heads in the oven.'

So it's that bad. Bad enough for me to come away from the exit, bad enough for me to venture back across the threadbare carpet and put my hand on Angel's shoulder. Bad enough even to pretend it can ever come right again.

'Tell me about Cameron, Ange.'

Turns out Cameron's the Mr Clean of racing. On the one hand, you got corruption, and on the other you got Cameron. I know a bit about him. There was a divorce, and an estrangement from a sister. He ended up in racing.

'Cyril was riding for him the day of the … Anyway, Cameron paid for Cyril's surgery and the prosthesis and the term in rehab. He said he didn't want anything in return but Cyril felt obligated. Which was one of the reasons he started gambling. Cameron –'

I rein her in. 'Tell me about the – accident.' She's got me stumbling over the nomenclature now.

She nods in the half-light, and in the half-light the bangle on her wrist glimmers and I can pretend she still looks halfway like the woman she once was. 'It was Cyril's first ride on Lord Haw-Haw. I believe the horse was slated to become the next Phar Lap. Anyway, Cameron instructed Cyril to ride to win – although Cyril doubted that the horse could.'

'How come?'

Cyril answers out of the shadows. 'On his previous three outings, Lord Haw-Haw came last. It was like he had, well, even more lead in his saddlebags than the handicap he usually had to carry. You'd think his previous riders were a bunch of apprentices, when in reality they were veterans. It was a miracle there was never an inquiry. Lord Haw-Haw should have won every race he was entered in. But the day I rode him, he was rated so low no-one bothered putting money on him – nobody except Cameron. Believe it or not, the magnificent Lord Haw-Haw was a rank outsider, with a starting price of fifty to one. Only Cameron had faith in him, and stood to make a mint if he won.'

It's a long speech, as long as Cyril can manage. He leans against the dame, clutching his toy horse so tightly it looks like its eyes are going to pop.

Angel takes up the baton. 'Except that, as we all know' – she shudders – 'Lord Haw-Haw didn't win.'

I remember, but I let her go on. It stops me thinking about Imogene.

'Cameron, Lord Haw-Haw's owner, a man who never lost on anything, was sure that Lord Haw-Haw was going to win. His last minute instructions to Cyril were to go for it. Cyril was to position the horse in third place until they came into the straight, after which he was to come down on the outside and win. That's what Cameron said, *ride to win*.'

Chapter 11

THE YELLOW CROSS

Angel shrugs her shoulders. 'Cameron wasn't – isn't – a man to bet against his own horse. It wasn't surprising, then, that he instructed Cyril to win. Except that –'

Even in the gritty light, I can see the anguish in her face. But beyond that, I see her bouncing up and down in the connections stand, the eyes of the other punters not on the race but on her, splendid in her frock and fascinator, eyes agleam with anticipation because she knows her husband is going to win. Instead of which –

'At the turn, Cyril was nicely tucked into third. He wasn't botoxed-in, or even in any danger of it, but riding sweetly with Lord Haw-Haw striding out ...'

Cyril nods. 'He had it in him. You can feel it when it's like that. There's a sensation under you like – like –'

Angel pats his arm. 'Go ahead, darling, you can say it – like a good woman. That's what you used to say to me. *You're just like a good horse, darling.* She turns back to me. 'I always took it as a compliment. After all, Cyril is – or rather, was – a great jockey.'

Cyril scratches himself again; he's close to tears as the dame comes into the straight and says how, with

200 metres to go, and with the jockeys all standing in their saddles, Cyril takes a tumble, Lord Haw-Haw goes down with him, and the entire field …

'It was my fault. I fell. How come a first-rate jockey falls? It was …'

How it looks to Angel from up in the stands is that every horse is trampling her man into the turf after his mount rolls off him. How horse and rider are still lying prone as the rest of the field thunders across the finish line.

'The upshot being that Cameron did his dough.' Angel hugs herself. 'Something happened. Cameron had told Cyril to win and he put a lot of money on the nose. So it couldn't have been Cameron.' A faraway look comes into her eyes. 'Anyway, he's not like that.'

That's when I figure there's something she's not telling me. I don't like it when there's something somebody's not telling me. Especially a client. Especially a non-paying one.

'It sounds like this Cameron meant a whole lot more to you than someone your husband once rode for.'

Angel's complexion turns a shade of raspberry. It's the sort of inner-glow that derives from heat, or lust, or simply the embarrassment that comes with guilt. 'I – he – we …'

Cyril's voice is savage. 'The bastard seduced her. It was Angel's way of paying off my debts. After things started going wrong, I developed the recklessness of the loser.' His mouth twists like he's got a shiff in his guts. 'But Cameron came to our rescue. So, yeah, I guess I owed him.'

Angel's knitting her hands together like she's making a jumper. 'He was so nice to us. He said it didn't matter. He said that he could afford to bail us out. But I told him I didn't like being in debt. So he said why not cut out the debt by – nothing sordid – but one thing led to another. I was still – pretty then, and looked a lot younger than my years.'

'And the debt?'

'The debt seemed to disappear into thin air after we started – going out.'

'How convenient.'

'When we – made love – it was only ever going to be a one-off.' She's having difficulty breathing. 'The trouble was that just as Cyril's gambling became a habit, so did my arrangement with Cameron. Then one day Cyril came to ask Cameron for money to put on a sure thing and discovered us …'

I glance at Cyril lurking in the shadows. It's not hard to guess how he reacted. 'What happened then?'

'I realised that my love for Cyril was great enough for me to let him go on getting into debt, but not enough for me to go on sleeping with Cameron to get him out of it.'

'So what happened to the gambling debts?'

'They were – amalgamated.'

I feel like I'm in a place of the condemned. If we were in the Dark Ages, this would be a domicile of the Doomed. In the Year of the Plague, the joint would have a yellow cross on the door.

'Going back, you said quote, unquote: *Cameron seemed to think Lord Haw-Haw would win.* What did you mean by that?'

'I meant that – for possibly the first time in his life – Cameron hadn't been in control.'

'Right. One last question, and this one's for you, Cyril. Who went down first – you or the horse?'

Cyril scratches himself as he ponders the question. 'It was me,' he says at last. 'I went down first.'

I go to squeeze Angel's arm but find little more in my fingers than skin and bone. 'Try and keep him out of the clutches of the nasties, okay, Ange?'

I let her go and the dame nods. There's something like hope in her sunken eyes, or maybe it's just the darkness. 'I'll try.'

I'm no betting man, but I'd lay good money against her chances.

Chapter 12

THE GAMBOLLING MAN

I manage to lose the dame in the leopardskin leotards (I know it's not Pandora, Pandora wears black) by cutting through the traffic, darting behind a 327 omnibus, turning a high-flying leap into a three-spin roll, and finally banging through the mob halfway between Books on King and a cut-price shoe shop.

On the other side of the Harbour, at the counter of the empty caff under a sign saying *TWO-UP COFFEE – THE ODDS ARE IT'S GREAT*, Harry Hopman's in residence, looking even wiser than usual. But the hand carrying the muck that passes for coffee in his establishment is shaking. Harry always shakes. He says it's with merriment, only he hasn't got much to be merry about.

'How they hanging, Harry?'

'By a thread.' He drops the mess of caffeine in front of me. 'But on the bright side, I could be dead tomorrow.' He chucks me a glance. 'How about you?'

I debate whether to try the coffee. Enjoying Harry's company doesn't mean I got to die doing it. 'Depends which side you're on.' I shrug. 'I just scored another non-paying customer and I'm in danger of losing Imogene. Otherwise everything's great. But I'm not here to complain.'

'No, you're here for my excellent coffee.'

'That, too.' I take a sip to show there's no ill feeling, but immediately wish I hadn't. 'Tell me, what do you know about the current state of horseracing?'

Harry used to be a bookie. 'Ask me something I don't know.' He wipes his nose on his apron and seats himself. 'In a word, once upon a time it was corrupt. Since then, only the names have changed.'

'What form does it take?'

He spreads his hands and looks at me like I was born tomorrow. 'Mate, your question should read: *What form doesn't it take?*' The sunlight picks out the life scars on his face. 'Trainers manipulate form, bookies bribe anyone that'll take their dosh, jockeys bet on nags they're racing against, stewards turn a blind eye to obstruction, and every other day a new drug's invented that doesn't show up on a swab.'

Harry's entitled to feel bitter. His missus left him for a female impersonator, his only kid's a junkie, and he lost his bookie's ticket for refusing to agree to a fix.

'Nice coffee, Harry.'

'Thanks, Rain.'

'Nice, too, the way the clouds form themselves into shapes. See that one over there to the left, there, above that mansion, the one with all the curlicues on it? Looks like a pig's snout.'

Harry doesn't look up. 'So what's your question?'

I come down out of the clouds and back to Harry. His coffee's crap but that doesn't mean his advice is. 'I want to know what – if any – organisation is involved. These people you're referring to – are they freelancers or is there some kind of logic to it – mafia, triads, bikers?'

Harry wipes his face like he's using his beard as a pumice. His five-o'clock shadow comes into contention five minutes after he shaves. 'Those groups you mention are into everything. This is the age of non-discrimination. This is a free-enterprise society meaning corruption is freely open to all.'

I knuckle the table. It's solid, but the answer isn't. 'You haven't answered my question.'

After Harry lost his bookie's ticket, he wasn't worth a brass razoo. A miracle payout on one of my jobs helped get him this hole-in-the-wall café. It's not worth anything, either, but that's the way he likes it. In a sad kind of way, he's a happy man. He examines his fingernails. They're dirty. 'You know the biggest beneficiary of gambling in this state? The government. On the one hand, they say we shouldn't do it, and on the other they're running TABs and lotteries and getting massive rake-offs from everything from pokies to scratchies. Not to mention sport.'

'So government equals corruption?'

Harry shrugs. 'I'm saying, seek and ye shall find. Because in the end, it all depends on what you're looking for.'

I lean back. The clouds still resemble pigs. 'Come on, mate. I'm looking for an answer to a conundrum. Let's try another tack. What do you know about a racing identity called Cameron?'

'Justin Cameron? The guy that owns racecourses?'

'Mate, no-one owns racecourses in this country.'

Harry picks up a copy of *The Daily Terrorgraph* that looks like it was mauled by a pack of dingoes. He riffles past stories about footballers throwing games in return for sex and cricket players throwing away sex in return for a game of cricket, and comes to a spread of a tall, smiley-faced gent in front of a Rolls-Royce and a racetrack. The headline reads:

FOR CAM THE MAN LIFE IN THE FAST LANE'S
NOTHING MORE THAN A GAMBOL

Harry waves the rag like he's just dropped a handline in a puddle and come up with a five-pound flounder. 'This one does.' He pauses for breath.

'Late last year, this very same rag ran a story on a guy that spent $10 million on a Formula One racetrack on the NSW Central Coast – five kilometres of road on five hectares of land.' Harry smacks the paper. 'This story says that your Justin Cameron is to racehorses what that bloke is to F1.'

I check out the photograph. This is the joker Angel was talking about. He's tall – close to my height. Except that, unlike me, he's got what you'd call class – pressed shirt, nice cravat, beautifully-tailored threads – and a smile that looks like it was put there by a surgeon. But it's the way he's standing that really impresses. Photographs usually diminish people but this guy diminishes the photograph. He's not smiling at the camera, the camera's smiling at him. And the Rolls-Royce by the racetrack looks like a toy.

'Impressive.'

Harry shoots me a glance. 'I know what you're

thinking, Rain – that's he's not exactly your shot of vodka. That doesn't make him any worse than anyone else. Get a load of this.'

Harry shows me another picture, this time accompanied by a bunch of statistics, under the heading:

ROYAL CAM-WICK

Circumference of Track, 2224 metres

Width of Track, 30 metres

Length of Straight, 410 metres

Width of Straight at Winning Post, 18 metres

Everything everyone doesn't need to know about Randwick Racecourse, and then some. So the man owns a track just like Randwick, so what? I plonk down the mug. 'What do you put in this coffee, Harry? Toadstools?'

'It's state of the art, Rainbow. Just like Cam the Man's track.'

'Yeah, and just as likely to give you the trots.' But I'm not here to do a commentary on the coffee. 'Tell me what else you know about Cam the Man.'

Chapter 13

THE SKELETON AT THE TABLE

Harry parks himself back in his seat and squints into the clouds.

I know why he serves such bad coffee. It's to keep the customers away, so he can sit and squint into the clouds. What I don't know is what drives Justin Cameron.

'Well, he's a big man.'

'I can tell that just by looking at the photo. How about telling me something I don't know?'

Harry drops his head between his shoulders. I call it his bird-of-prey look, only anyone less like a bird of prey would be harder to pick than a winner at Randwick. 'We both know about losers, Rain. Losers are your day-to-day everyman. It's a word that carries plenty of connotations but means nothing. Everyone's a loser in my book and there's nothing wrong with that. Losers are just the people that admit it.'

'Only this joker doesn't?'

He shakes his head. If everyone's a loser, Harry's a winner among losers. Everything's gone wrong in his life – family, fortune and reputation – but somehow he always comes up smoking daisies. 'No,

Cameron wins and that's his problem. He doesn't have to buy politicians, they fawn over him without his paying them a sou. He knows racing backwards. And – until recently, anyway – he always backed winners.'

I forget the coffee. I forget Imogene and the fact I'm on the cusp of losing her. I even forget the shadow that's flitting among the trees down the road.

'What do you mean – *until recently?*'

'Just what I said, *until recently.*'

'How recently?'

'About two years recently.'

'Cameron's been losing for two years?' I tap the blatt. 'He doesn't look like he's losing here.'

'The *Terrorgraph* specialises in old photos.'

'Okay, so tell me how come he's losing. Is it the Global Financial Casuistry? His investments going bad? Cards not falling the way they should?'

'None of the above. Cameron's a specialist. He only does racing, and then only one kind of racing. Not the doggies, not the trots – not even camels or cane toads. He's Justin Cameron and with him it's just gallopers.' Harry shrugs. 'Hence the beautiful, turfed racetrack you see on the table before you.'

'So what happened?'

Harry gazes at me out of eyes that go back to the beginning of time. 'My guess is that something leapt out of his past at him. Some folk call it karma.'

I feel my skull contract. 'Why do you think that?'

Harry shrugs. 'Because there's no other explanation for his misfortune.'

I bring myself back to the main line. The clouds

have turned back into clouds, and I remind myself that the only reality you can rely on in this world is the facts. 'So tell me about the beautiful, turfed racetrack.'

Harry raises an eyebrow. 'What's there to tell? It's on a slab of land carved out of rainforest south of Sydney. And like the newspaper says, it's built along exactly the same lines as Randwick – same size, same dimensions, same layout. I suppose Cameron organises private races on it. No law against that. A little something for the man who has everything.'

'And?'

'And what?'

'There's always an and.'

Harry climbs to his feet, revealing the fact that he's in about the same physical condition as a thousand-year-old mummy. 'You're the detective, Rain. I'm just an ordinary, everyday coffee mechanic. Show me a field of horses and all I see is the colour of the silks on the jockeys riding them. To me and to the rest of the world, Justin Cameron's exactly what he appears to be – a winner.'

I decline a second cup of coffee. To accept might put me in the same physical state as Harry. So I stand, jam on the chapeau, kick the chair back under the table, and before leaving, chuck a final glance at the blatt. Down in the bottom right-hand corner, I notice an ad for some bunch going by the name MRS GRUNDY, featuring a skeleton crouched at a card table with – standing apart and looking on – a beautiful dame with a concerned smile on her dial-up and a comic-strip word bubble coming out of her mouth:

Gambling a problem?
Why not pay us a visit?
Followed by an address, a website and a telephone number.

My way back to the *Wooden No* leads past the kid. Today, tomorrow and forever, my way back to anywhere is going to lead past the kid. I knock on the door of the joint on Castanet Close and Salina answers.

'What are you doing here?' Her fingers tighten on the door knob.

'I just wanted to see the kid.'

'Well, you can't see the kid.'

'I need to remind her that I exist.'

'And I want to remind her that you don't.'

Maybe I'm imagining the movement in the hallway. 'Is there someone there with you?'

'Yes, my daughter, Imogene.'

'Anyone else?'

'Like everything in my life from now on, Rainbow, that's for me to know and you not to find out.'

I turn away.

It's the kid that matters, my feelings don't butter parsnips.

I got to find a distraction.

I got a name for the distraction.

Justin Cameron.

Chapter 14

DEATH BY OVERSIGHT

Pandora's in abeyance but the tail's still in place, a dame in colourful leotards – sometimes patterned, sometimes plain, but always colourful – behind trees, in shop doorways, lurking on the other side of cars, half-merging with the crowd, but never quite making it. She's an inept follower. Which is why I don't try to double back on her. Why bother? She's easy to see, easier still to lose. She's been with me, on and off, since I first stumbled on that stiff at Central. Since then, another body has been found with the same tell-tale marks: slight contusions, cuts, burns and abrasions. According to the so-called news reports – paragraphs that are no more than fillers – the fuzz aren't too interested, content with merely filing the corpses under a generic that might read 'Death by Societal Oversight', and leaving it to people like Annie to dispose of the remains.

I shake the dame that's following me at Pimlico's, heading through the billiard room, out through the end window – the one with the rock 'n' roll lock on half-cock and the cut-price surround – and down the side alley. After that, I get myself to Rube's.

'It's been a while, Rainbow.'

'Sorry, Aunt. I been busy.'

She's cased me through the peephole and now she's standing in the doorway of her Darlinghurst down-at-heel, checking right and left along the boulevard like she always does, scrawny as a bug-empty stocking, but still capable of taking on the world.

'No need for excuses.'

There's barely enough of her to throw a shadow as she precedes me down the hall.

'I could lose Imogene, Rube.'

We're in her kitchen, a place full of blue china and memories.

She shrugs. 'Everyone loses their kids at some point. If you bet against that, you'd put your life savings on a grass seed in a whirlwind.'

'I haven't got any life savings.'

'It's just an expression.'

'Right.' Rube's coffee is better than Harry's. Then again, mud's better than Harry's. I backhand my mouth. 'So what do I do?'

'Focus on the job. From what you're telling me, Sal's found herself a fella. Let the dust settle. The kid can work out how it goes from here.'

'What if he's dangerous?'

Rube inclines her head. 'That dame can look after herself.'

'I'm not worried about Sal.'

'Then ditto the kid.'

For once I reckon Rube's only half-right. It could be because I'm jumping at shadows. Then again, it could be because Rube's only half-right. I down my mug of caffeine and watch my past dance around the walls – ballet, ethics, music, detection methods, James Cagney movies, escapology.

'You know, you're too close to the action, Rainbow. With everything in this life, you got to ignore the bones and consider the skeleton. Just because the occipital's a long way from the tarsus doesn't mean ...'

Rube's voice trails off and after I've used her computer, so do I.

I don't need a sniffer dog to locate Phoebe Riesling because, one: the name of her current employer's familiar; two: she's not trying to hide from anyone; and three: the joint where she works is located in sunny Newtown, just around the corner from Cyril's hovel. I find Phoebe at a honey-coloured desk in the front room of a yellow-painted terrace.

'I'd like to speak with your boss.'

She chucks me a glance out of the hard eyes, says she'll be with me shortly, then goes back to whatever she was doing before I showed up, leaving me to check out my surroundings.

Cramped reception room that feels even more cramped on account of all the signs in it. *MRS GRUNDY INC.* reads the plaque over the yellow door behind the dame. And underneath:

We're not concerned with being what we're not, and not afraid to be what we are.

After I've given up trying to work out that little gem, I discover it's open slather on epigrams.

Give away gambling, not your money
Family first, last and always
Trust in God, not man
Tobacco or not tobacco – hardly a question
Drink for Thirst, Don't Thirst for Drink

And more obscurely:

We might live in a yellow submarine, but that doesn't mean we have to go down with the others

Posters cover every available inch of space. Shots of happy families, pictures of sad ones. Crosses for stubbies of beer and ticks for what look like bottles of Vichy water. Brisk walks are in, wild parties out. Hard work's favoured. So is neck-to-knee swimwear. All very interesting, but after five minutes of wallowing in holy water I'm done.

'Have you pressed any buttons yet, lady?'

Phoebe Riesling shakes her coif and nails me with her sharp-pointed eyes. 'I said I'd be with you shortly. So in the meantime, would you mind taking a seat? You're making me nervous.'

'Yeah, I would mind as a matter of fact. I also mind standing around doing nothing but read *Aesop's Fables*.' I nod at the door behind her. 'You got a boss tucked away in there somewhere. Get her for me.'

'All in good time.'

I shake my head. 'No, all in bad time, lady.' I move a step closer.

She shrinks back. 'Really, this is most improper.'

'Life's most improper, get used to it. What you did with my kid was most improper. And if you don't find your boss for me in a hurry, I'll most improperly bust down that door behind you and most improperly find her myself.'

Chapter 15

MRS GRUNDY SAYS

When Phoebe's boss appears, she's sporting a nice hairdo, nice white, sensible, surgical-type footwear, white gloves, white frock and stockings – and the sort of face that's usually worn by a shop window dummy or a nun: perfect, composed and flawless.

'I believe you have a problem.'

Under the carefully coiffed hair, the peepers coolly take me apart. I take my own eyes for a return tour of the signs on the walls, before bringing them back to the dame at the door.

'I was just wondering …'

She manages the kind of smile that's not going to do permanent damage to the flawless complexion, but does a lot of damage to me. 'I thought so. All right, let's talk about it, shall we?' She glances at her colleague behind the desk. 'Thank you for notifying me, Miss Riesling, you did the right thing.' A curt nod is thrown in my direction. 'Now, if you'll just follow me.'

I keep my mind on what Rube told me while I follow the dame. Keep your eye on the big picture. So I keep my eye on the big picture, and the big picture tells me that under the white gloves and all her get-up and go-for-it, this dame's really something. After that, I try to forget the beautiful calves, the promise of fine strength in the lithe body under all the starched whiteness, and the wasp waist.

'Would you like to sit?'

I remove my fedora and sit as she pirouettes easily and calmly on her sensible shoes before leaning back and pressing the appropriate part of her anatomy against the edge of her desk. At the same time she crosses her arms and fixes me with eyes of the same cold blue as the water at Bondi this morning. 'I don't believe we've met, Mr er –'

'You don't believe right. The name's Brown, John Brown.'

'Fancy that.' It's like she was expecting an invention and what I just gave her was pretty much what she expected. 'Perhaps you could provide me with a few details.'

Her room's much like the one outside – minimal furniture, a window that looks onto a brick wall, and possessing about as much ambience as a mausoleum.

'And maybe you could, too,' I say. 'Like, for starters, what's with the "Mrs Grundy" caper?'

She eases herself off the desk and for a moment I get the wildest of fancies she's going to hurl herself at me. But it proves to be no more than a sad case of the wistfuls, because instead, she dusts imaginary dust off her gloves, moves back behind her desk, and sits, and there are still no creases in the perfect complexion when she smiles.

'It's just a little fancy of mine, Mr Brown. Mrs Grundy is, of course, a fiction – a character in a play by someone named Morton called *Speed the Plough*.'

Speed the Plough did the rounds of theatres in

Merrie Olde Englande something like two hundred years ago. I know the story but I need to see where this is going, so I let her tell me.

'Mrs Grundy was the neighbour everyone worries about. People would ask: *What will Mrs Grundy say?* Of course, Mrs Grundy was a figure of fun – that's what she became, anyway – but I believe she represents everything that's good in this world. Mrs Grundy is *morality.*'

So now we got a morality play on our hands.

'When I was setting up my organisation and looking for a name, I decided to adopt hers. Because in the same way as Mrs Grundy, we stand for what's good in this world, and we're not afraid to admit it.'

'So you became Mrs Grundy.'

'I suppose it sounds silly, but, yes, that's who I became.' She cuts across my thoughts. 'Look, I know what you're thinking – that Grundies are no more than people who don't mind their own business.' She shrugs. 'But don't you think, Mr – Brown – that sometimes other people's business needs minding? If only for their own good?'

'Yeah, like, for instance, when my daughter was minding her own business earlier today and you and your colleague out there decided to abduct her.'

The dame frowns. 'Do refresh my memory, please. Exactly what business was your daughter minding, and where?'

I do the pause most people do before they come out with half-truths. 'She was at Darling Harbour, in the city.'

She caresses her throat with one of her gloved hands. 'Whereabouts at Darling Harbour, in the city?' She has a pen in her hand and she's writing something with it, and her body – at least what I can see of it above the desk – has a kind of hard-edged wiriness about it. The clothing doesn't do her justice. Then again, maybe I'm not doing her justice.

'The northern end.'

'That would have been on the steps outside the casino?'

She's got me on the back foot. I don't like being on the back foot. 'Look, she just happened to be waiting for me.'

'And how old is this this daughter of yours who just happened to be waiting for you?'

'She's – I –'

She strokes her beautiful throat with her white-gloved hand. 'I see. So you don't even know the age of this much-loved daughter of yours. And I suppose you were just visiting old friends in the Star.' The gloved hand stops its stroking and returns to the desktop alongside the other one with the pen. 'Mr Brown, let's stop pussy-footing around, shall we? Gambling is bad enough without also leaving your child at the mercy of an uncertain populace.'

After forcing my way in here, I had no chance of winning this dame's affections. Now I got even less. I take a deep breath – the kind I usually take before putting my head under water. 'My daughter was in no danger, except from people like you. Now, as a direct result of your actions – to whit, removing my kid from where I safely left her and taking her back to her mother, thereby implying that I'm a bad father – I'm probably going to lose her on a more or less permanent basis.'

She puts down her pen, stands, and moves across to the window that overlooks the brick wall. 'But if you're a gambler, Mr Brown, don't you think you deserve to lose your child?'

'Yeah, except that I'm not a gambler. So on your reasoning, I don't. It's no business of yours, anyway, except that you made it that way. For the record I wasn't gambling, I was rescuing someone who was. So it looks like I might be in the same business as you.'

'I see.'

'No, I'm not sure you do. You think you got a mortgage on uprightness. The cops are bad enough, but you?' I hunch the shoulders, then I unhunch them. 'You think you got all the answers, when in actual fact, you're part of the problem.'

She turns and faces me. 'All right, all right, you've made your point.' The voice is suddenly gentle and I'm suddenly in love again. 'Exactly what do you want me to do?'

This is what I'm here for. 'I want you to pay a visit to my ex-wife and tell her you acted prematurely. That her – our – kid wasn't abandoned, that you and your colleague only thought she was. That you're convinced I wasn't neglectful, and nor was I gambling. That you made an honest mistake, and that you're of the honest opinion that me and the kid shouldn't have to pay for it.'

She comes up close to where I'm sitting, and this time when she smiles, it looks like it might almost be real. 'I'd be more than happy to revisit your ex-wife, Mr Brown,' she purrs. 'And let me add that I'm genuinely sorry for any inconvenience Miss

Riesling and I might have caused. We take our work very seriously. As a result we sometimes get a little carried away.'

As I get up to go, I got one last question. Always ask the last question. 'What is your work exactly?'

She moves away, like somehow it's safer, and maybe she's right. 'Clearly you don't read the women's magazines.' She's back behind the desk. 'In an eggshell, I run a well-known and highly-respected charity set up to help people with problems, particularly in the fraught area of gambling. And to help me, I employ what are generally known as *fallen women ...*'

Chapter 16

WHERE THERE'S SMOKE ...

I think outside the square – and beyond the room – to Phoebe Riesling in the foyer. It makes sense. Something bad can sometimes lead to good.

'Oh, yeah,' I say, 'I understand – *the harlot's cry* I believe the poet called it, something to do with *the whore and the gambler ...*'

'Oh, for goodness' sake, Mr Whatever-your-name-is, I'm not using fallen women in that sense. The women who work for me aren't ex- whatever they're called these days – sex-workers. No, I'm talking about women who have been irrevocably hurt, usually in their own homes. Women who have had the ground cut out from under them by – some person or other. Women who – I give those women a chance to be –'

'I get the picture.'

She recovers her equipoise. 'Let's just say I find such women make excellent assistants. And before you ask how we manage to keep ourselves in such luxury, as far as the running costs of our organisation are concerned, benefactors make donations, while others pay us to help rescue their loved ones from whatever their problem might be.' She throws me a look out of her Bondi-blue eyes.

'Perhaps there's something you'd like to contribute, Mr Brown?'

She's right.

There is.

But I slip her a ten-spot instead.

The joker that ducks into the government-run Totalisator Agency Betting place – all right, the TAB – just as I emerge from the Grundy pad looks familiar. So does the figure that follows the joker in, a black-clad male in cowboy boots known around the traps as Bat Masterson – or just plain Batty. Bat's an enforcer, a thug sent out into the wilderness by persons to whom the debts owing are owed to collect. Call him a commission agent. Call him dangerous.

A siren sounds in the distance, so it must be lunchtime, and the TAB's in full swing so it must be Thursday, the day when punters are dealt the dole and can't wait for the chance to hand it straight back to the people that gave it to them. I haul out the gat. This is the inner city. Once, it was prostitutes, razor gangs and bent police, but now it's mostly gambling, and the cops stay home and do paperwork in the office, because gambling's legal. The barred-window terraces could be cells in a maximum-security prison, the four-wheel-drives outside look all set for a tour of duty in Afghanistan, and the sirens are echoing in company with the unmistakeable smell of smoke as I ease myself inside.

Sure enough, I see two figures at the grilled window, while the face with the fake smile on the television screen perched on its dinky little shelf among all the racing ads is introducing the next race at Royal Randwick.

'The track favours the cleanskins, so the smart money's on The Mole.'

Cyril's clutching his pony and I get close enough to the action to realise that Bat Masterson goes through life without the benefit of deodorant.

Cyril shoves a sheaf of notes through the grille. 'A hundred on The Mole.'

Batty shoves Cyril aside and palms the dough-re-me. 'This gentleman's not betting today,' he advises the grille.

'I would have thought that was for the gentleman to decide,' the grille replies.

'And I would of thought you'd shut your cakehole.'

The grille purses its mouth and Cyril shrugs. 'I guess I'm not betting today.'

Batty's got one hairy hand on Cyril's shoulder. 'I want everything you've got,' he snarls, 'and then some.'

'I haven't got anything!'

'Mate, you were just about to bet a motza.'

'But the money's not mine.'

'You're dead right it's not yours.' The rest of the punters keep their heads down as the thug shovels Cyril past the television towards the exit. 'And neither is your life if you don't hand over the rest of what you owe us.'

'Look, I'll pay you, I promise.'

'I don't do promises.'

The television goes into overdrive. '... *but The Mole's come nowhere! The favourite ...*'

Batty spins on his high heels. 'Turn the bastard off.'

'I'm sorry, but the television's on automatic,' says the grille.

'And so am I.' Batty reaches up and punches the TV's on/off button and the screen goes black. He turns back to Cyril. 'Hand over the goodies, Cyril, or you're next.'

Another siren sounds outside – this time louder – and Batty flinches. I think he realises the jig might be up and that today he's going to have to leave empty-handed. He lets go and on his way out gives me a bad look.

I seize the opportunity and grab Cyril.

'Hey, you're hurting me!'

'Stop struggling or I'll hurt you some more. Now move it.'

We get ourselves into an old drainage way where the smell of smoke has just got even stronger.

'Handy, isn't it – having a betting parlour just around the corner from the hovel you've reduced Angel to.' I give him a shake; I feel like giving him a lot more. 'So what was that all about?'

Cyril hugs his toy horse. 'It was a cop car.'

'I'm not talking about the sirens, you moron, I'm talking about the joker in the Roy Orbison outfit. He work for the people you owe the money to?'

'One of them.'

'So how many are there?'

'Heaps.'

When I shake him, it's the horse's teeth that rattle. 'How much do you owe the people that Batty works for?'

'By my reckoning, nothing. The horse they told me would win just came last. How can that be owing anyone?'

'You're using the wrong logic, pal. If a bloke like that says you owe him, then you owe him, and if you want to stay alive, you pay him.'

Cyril's shoulders slump even lower than they are already. 'I can't afford to pay anyone anything.'

The smell of smoke keeps getting stronger. 'Then you can't afford to stay alive.'

Chapter 17

... THERE'S MURDER

If I'd been concentrating on the big picture instead of rescuing Cyril, I'd have known who the sirens belonged to: the firies. As we turn into Cyril's street, punters up and down the boulevard are gaping at the action and the hoses are spreadeagled all over the carriageway. There's too much water on the tar-macadam and far too much smoke in the atmosphere.

Lord Haw-Haw grimaces as Cyril hardens his grip on him. 'Jesus, if it's not one thing it's another!'

I resist strangling him. 'Wrong, pal.' I haul him out of the way of a fireman struggling past with a hose. 'This is not another thing because what just happened is all part of the same thing. And that thing is that you're an inveterate gambler who's wallowing in his own misery. That's the real reason you got no funding, the heavies are onto you, you're living in a hole, and it just burnt down. It's also – if we stretch the actuality – why I'm in danger of losing my daughter.' A thought suddenly hits me. 'Where is she?'

'Who, your daughter?'

I tear my eyes away from the blackened remains of the shack and the firemen packing up their trucks, and plant them on Cyril. 'No, you idiot, your wife!' I shake him. 'Was she at home?'

Cyril does his bent-shouldered shrug, and the toy horse shrugs with him. 'How would I know?'

'She's your wife!'

Something seems to stir in his memory, but nothing moves in what's left of the hovel. 'I seem to remember something about her going to the pawn shop on King Street. Something about a bangle.'

The hovel's a wreck, the firies have nearly finished putting away their hoses because there's nothing left to play them on, and the wet ashes glimmer like lost hope in the wan sunlight. I cast my eyes around the smoking cinders, fear in my heart. There's a broken cup, a charred table leg, a burnt sack of rubbish, a blackened shoe. I turn away and am confronted by the wreckage of the joker beside me.

'Cyril, do you even care?'

A cop car cruises by and I drag him into the crowd and out of the squaddie's sightline. This place is too hot for comfort. Aside from which, I suddenly – make that urgently – need to determine the last-known whereabouts of Angela Golightly.

'So where's this pawn shop?'

Hope springs eternal in Cyril's eyes. 'Why, you got something to flog?'

The pawn shop's a pawn shop – dusty guitars chained in the doorway like mangy kelpies, its next-door neighbour a brothel, and too full of the proceeds of crime for comfort.

A hairball adjusting the scenery frowns at Cyril's mangy horse. 'Youse can both piss off and take your shitty toy with you.'

You can't reason with usurers. I chuck a glance around the hock shop. 'We're looking for a woman.'

'Next door.'

'A specific woman.'

'Like I said, brothel's next door.'

I haul out the gat.

Hairball backs off. 'Just kidding.' He gets behind the counter. I watch the hands. He sees me watching the hands and keeps them away from the alarm bell, fingers spread like he's drying nailpolish. 'What's she look like, this woman you're after?'

'Brunette. Tall, blue eyes, skinny. Once beautiful, but that was before she fell victim to a husband that gambles.'

The usurer looks at Cyril. They know each other. 'This the husband?'

I put away the gat. 'Yeah.'

'And the woman's five-nine or thereabouts, whippet-thin, and answers to the name of Angela Golightly?'

I tell him *Yeah* again.

'Sorry, mate, ain't seen her since the day before yesterday.'

The firies and the crowd have dispersed. Where the hovel once stood there's nothing but a sodden pile of ashes, a bunch of witches' hats, a few lengths of red tape, the blackened remains of a sign that once read 'TOiLET', and a great deal of sadness. No cops, though. I suppose it was only a hovel.

I make my way into the sadness and the whitesides turn monochrome. The decay has been replaced by burnt decay. I clock a patch of threadbare carpet that somehow escaped the inferno, the collapsed remains of a kitchen sink that a couple of cockroaches once raced on, a charred shoe, and a large, blackened can.

Then I see the bangle. It's the one I gave a once-beautiful dame for saving me from post-marriage desuetude, a band of 32-carat gold with no strings attached that was tight on her arm when I gave it to her, but loose as a mug punter's morals when I saw it last time.

But that was last time.

At first I think it's just the smoke seeping up out of the wreckage that's getting in the way of my vision. Because everything's suddenly gone hazy – the brow-beaten walls, the charred rafters, the fallen-in, corrugated-tin roof and the still-smouldering remains of a once-beautiful dame.

I grab the bracelet and get the hell out of there.

Chapter 18

THE MATCHSTICK MAN

Outside, Cyril's hunched in the gutter clutching Lord Haw-Haw. There's soot smeared all over his white face, and his mumbling sounds like a snake slithering brittle-skinned over charred stubble after a grass fire.

But I got no grace left in me, and even less sympathy. 'Come on,' I say and drag him away from the ashes, the witches' hats, and Angel. 'That was your wife in there – or what was left of her after you and the conflagration had their way.'

He cringes as if expecting a beating. I don't do the physical, I hit him with the truth instead. 'Fact number one: she's dead. I wish it was you in her place, but the sad reality is that it isn't.'

I shake off the bad thoughts and the worse words, recalling the remains of the petrol can in what used to be the hovel's doorway. 'Fact number two: it was murder. Some matchstick man wanted to kill you but got your missus instead. It seems that your miserable life might have been saved by the intercession of the thug in the betting parlour, rendering you too late for your own funeral, but dumping Angel in the coffin instead.'

I stop, turn and face Cyril and what's left of his

conscience. 'And fact number three is I'm going to find out who did it, starting with your mate at the TAB. He could have been on the same team as the matchstick man, and it was all nothing but a monumental cock-up, a case of the right hand not knowing what the wrong hand was doing.'

Cyril's eyes glaze over. I don't know if he's worked out he's a widower, or he's just thinking about the next race.

'So who's Bat Masterson working for? Who was into you for money?'

'I – I don't know. Jesus wept!' Tears spring to his eyes and his mouth quivers. 'It could have been – anyone.' He shakes his head. 'I owed so many people. I know it sounds bad, but it seems like there wasn't anyone I didn't owe money to.' His frown is shared by his toy horse as he squeezes it. 'But why would anyone want to kill me? I was going to make a – a killing. And they'd all get their money back. They'd get nothing from me dead.'

That's when a new thought strikes me. 'Did anyone want to kill Angel?'

Cyril stares at me. 'Who'd want to kill Angela?' His eyes brim. 'She was a – a – a –'

I shake him. 'Keep it together, mate, you owe it to her. Tell me the name of your major creditor.'

Cyril shakes his head. It's like it's all finally got to him. 'Jesus, I feel – down.' His feet shuffle on the footpath and if his shoulders were any more bowed he wouldn't possess any. He sags back into the gutter like a sack of suet, parking the horse on the kerb beside him. 'I feel like topping myself.'

'Well, would you delay the process until we find

out who killed your missus? After which, you can do what you like as far as I'm concerned, as long as it doesn't involve killing anyone else.'

He frowns. 'Hey, wait a minute, I remember now. I amalgamated all my debts.'

'Who to?'

He shakes his head. 'I – I don't know. Someone approached me one day and said they'd amalgamate my debts and I said okay.'

'People don't just –'

He shakes his head again. 'This one did. And I agreed. I mean, why not? If someone's silly enough to –'

'Was it by any chance Cameron?'

'No, like I said before, Cameron was losing, too. My fall was part of it.'

'Part of what?'

'Jesus, all these questions! How do you expect me to know? Part of the big picture I'm trying to paint for you, but I'm only a tiny part of it.'

'Okay, okay. Back to Cameron: where do I find him?'

'Probably at his club.'

'And which club might that be?'

'They call it the Residence, but it's by invitation only.'

I dump Cyril at O'Leary's – the speakeasy that doesn't exist on Patterson – slipping Hank the barman my last fifty to keep an eye on him, in case he decides to honour his threat. I then make my way to Club Privilege. The joint's on Castlereagh Street in an edifice thrown up in Queen Victoria's time to make Sydney look like an integral part of the Empire – all sandstone and marble and Corinthian columns – and while it takes twenty minutes to get there, it takes a whole lot longer to get past the flunky in the highly-polished doorway.

'I'm sorry, sir, but you can't come in dressed like that.'

I'm wearing the candy-coloured coat teamed with the red tie, green strides, whitesides, and the all-purpose fedora, and the gat's not apparent – even if you were looking for it.

'Dressed like what?'

'We have a dress code, sir, and in about a hundred and one ways you don't even begin to conform to it.'

'I'd prefer we not get hung up over wardrobes.'

'A lot of us would prefer a whole lot of things in this life, sir, but it doesn't mean we get them.'

Chapter 19

A MATTER OF GILT

Out on the street, a Rolls-Royce Silver Spoon disgorges a dame wearing what looks like a close-knit family of dead wombats around her neck. She waltzes up the staircase without being challenged over the marsupials, and a joker in a top hat and green livery bows so low he almost licks her Gucci-clad hoofs. This woman is alive, while Angela's as dead as egalitarianism.

I try a different tack. 'I'm here to see one of your members.'

The flunky's got the courage of his connections. 'Look, I'm sorry, sir, but I very much doubt if any of our members would know someone like you.'

I square the shoulders. 'They mightn't know me, but they'll know what I'm here for.'

'I very much doubt that, too.'

'It concerns the death of a mutual friend.'

'So go advertise it in the newspapers.'

'I'm not handing out invitations to a funeral.'

A bunch of tourists has noticed the altercation and is busy bringing out the cameras. I don't like cameras, never have. I hunch my back to them.

'I'm coming in.'

'Not if I can help it.'

'You can't help it.'

I'm out of the firing line and into the foyer, where I find an expensive carpet, a lot of chandeliers and too much mahogany.

The goon's followed me and lays a heavy hand on my shoulder. 'This is as far as you get without giving me a name.'

'I don't give my name to nobody.'

'The name of a member.'

I give him the name of a member.

The name excites the minion. 'I'm sorry, sir, no-one sees Mr Cameron.'

I sense an advantage, so I press it home. 'Tell Mr Cameron the death I'm inquiring about is that of Angela Golightly.'

'I could tell him that, sir, but I don't see …'

'So go tell him, and don't bother looking.'

I have trouble breathing the air, it's that refined. A bellboy in a performing monkey's hat shows me to a room that's as dark as a murderer's thoughts – except instead of being a repository for guilt, it's full of gilt. The walls are designer green, the only lighting's by way of sconces, and the rest of the darkness comes courtesy of an expensive Axminster.

'I don't believe we've met.'

We're both on the upside of six feet, but after that, any resemblance is purely illusory. Justin Cameron is dressed in the sort of clobber only a great deal of money can buy and is wearing an expression that would be at home on the dial-up of Pope Francis. In contrast I'm dressed by Vinnies and possess a face crafted by too many maulings.

'The name's Black.'

'Black by name, black by nature, eh?' There's no handshake, and little else by way of welcome. 'Well, Mr Black, I can't say it's nice meeting you because that would be a lie. For a start, I don't know who or what you are.' He examines me through his aristocratic eyes. 'In fact, I don't even know why I agreed to let you in.'

'She's dead.'

I'm watching the face, but the darkness and the breeding prevent me seeing anything worth seeing.

'My good man, I don't believe we're – how might your sort of person put it? – reading from the same form guide.'

'Look, pal, I know for a fact that Angela Golightly was a friend of yours. I also know she's just died a gruesome and unjustified death.'

Cameron's features start to make sense in the gloom, and the sense they're making is that he's halfway listening. It's a start.

'By the time she was burned to death, Angel was so malnourished as a result of her husband's gambling it was a wonder there was anything left to burn.' I drag the bangle out of my poche. It glimmers dully in the dull light. 'She was wearing this at the time. It was just about all there was left of her.'

The bauble shows obvious signs of the fire and Cameron shows even more obvious signs of recognising it. Finally some emotion creeps into the Easter Island features. His fine hands drift up

to hide the features, and his voice is a whisper. 'My
God …'

The dame wearing the family of wombats around
her neck waltzes in. 'Oh, there you are.' She glances
at me. 'I was looking all over … And this would be?'

Cameron doesn't move, just stands there, hands
concealing his emotion. 'Be quiet, dear, and go
away, will you?'

Mrs Cameron – it's got to be Mrs Cameron –
obliges, like she was never there in the first place.
While his treatment of his fork-and-knife leaves a
lot to be desired, his reaction to the death of Angela
Golightly seems genuine enough.

I home in on the remorse, chagrin, mourning –
call it what you will. 'Someone killed her.'

'How do you know that?'

'I don't have to be Sherlock Holmes to know a
torch job when I see one.'

'A torch job?'

'Someone lit the fire deliberate, Cameron. And
Angel was home at the time.'

'But why would anyone want to kill her?'

'Because her husband's a compulsive gambler and
deep in debt.' I pause. 'I figured you might be the
one holding the promissory notes.'

Cameron shakes his head. 'I – I tried to help.'

'By seducing Angela and afterwards waiving a few
debts owed by the husband you cuckolded. It's a
good thing you were trying.'

'You don't understand.' He's right. I don't. 'Why kill Angela?'

'I figure whoever did it was after her husband and they just happened to hit the wrong target. Torches aren't known as people of great and unerring discernment.' I watch him up close and personal while I say it – my rods and cones have adjusted to the twilight – to determine if the distress really is genuine.

He takes his hands off his face. The distress really is genuine.

'And what's your interest in all this?'

'I'm an ordinary, everyday gumshoe, a nosy parker, a private eye who – like you – happens to have once been a lover of Miss Golightly's. And being what I am, by God I'm going to find out who murdered her.'

Chapter 20

A NICE LITTLE SHORT-CUT

I remember what I've learned about Justin Cameron, then I forget it, because it's always better to start with a clean slate.

He looks at me sharply. 'Why should I know anything?'

'Because her husband, Cyril Golightly, used to ride for you – until the accident. You seduced Angela Golightly. Following on from which, you're a big potato in the racing world. That all adds up to your being a prime suspect.'

I haven't been invited to sit in one of the buttoned-down leather couches dotting the room. I haven't even been invited to sit.

'That doesn't mean I killed her. Your evidence is hardly what you people might call damning.'

'Circumstantial will do to start with. I won't ask where you were at the time of Miss Golightly's death. Going by your hands, I'd say you're not the kind of person to get them dirty torching a tenement. But that doesn't mean you wouldn't pay someone else to do it for you.'

He winces. There are a lot of ways of reacting when you're guilty, and wincing isn't one of them. 'Look, Mr – Black, I feel just as strongly about this

– murder as you apparently do. Miss Golightly was a beautiful woman, in all senses of the word. And now that I know of her – passing – I will be paying for her funeral.' He considers me for a moment, but only for a moment. 'I would also like to retain your services in the matter, in the hope you might be able to discover the identity of the killer.'

'Why would you want to do that?'

'Because I didn't do it, and I want to know who did.'

'Or you did do it, and in hiring me, hope to convince the world that you didn't.'

'Except that I'd say that the world's not all that interested. Oh, people will eventually discover she's dead. And because she used to be someone, there'll be the usual kerfuffle in the tabloid press. But our lovely libel laws will keep them away. And the police are very careful with people like me.' He straightens the flapdoodles on the pockets of his expensive jacket. 'Do you want the job, or not?'

'I'm already doing the job. The question is do I want to take your money in order to do it.'

Cameron nods, but only slightly, like it's more of an effort than it's worth. 'Your principles are noteworthy, Mr Black, but princi*pal's* always more persuasive in these matters, I've found. Among the corrupt, money is a nice little short-cut to the finishing line. Of course, I'm in no way corrupt, but I suggest you're much more likely to solve a case when you possess the wherewithal to solve it.' He reaches into the breast pocket of his expensive jacket and withdraws a wad.

I grab the moolah and tuck it away. 'You've

convinced me.'

'Very well. Someone's dudding me. Someone's fixing the races.'

I remember what Harry Hopman told me about corruption. I frown at the big man lounging in the Chesterfield opposite me. 'Come on, pal, all races are fixed.'

Cameron makes the sort of gesture you can't buy in an opportunity shop. 'That's a hackneyed concept, if you don't mind my saying so. It may have been true once, but it's not so now. At least it wasn't until someone started it all up again a couple of years ago.'

'What do you mean – *it all*?'

'I mean, changing the pattern – altering the way races are run. Winners suddenly stopped being winners.'

'You mean the horses you were confident were going to win, stopped winning?'

He chucks me an aristocratic look, the kind that frowns on innuendos. 'What are you suggesting? There was nothing untoward in my knowledge. I'm an intelligent man. I simply apply that intelligence to racing.'

I move onto the next race on the card. 'Okay. Got any idea who's doing the fixing?'

'No idea. Only that once upon a time I could win.' He glances at me in the expensive gloom. 'But now I can't.'

I hunch the shoulders. 'All right, question one: how are races fixed?' I know the answer but I want it from the horse's mouth, or as near as I can get without being bitten.

'How long's a whip? For a start, there's dermorphin – otherwise known as frog juice, because somehow or other these scientific johnnies get the stuff out of frogs. Then there's etorphine – they call it elephant juice, or cobra venom …' He makes a gesture. 'It's a long list, because there are many ways. For instance, there are the painkillers, like the opioid analgesic butorphanol. Am I going too fast for you?'

'Not as fast as some of those ponies must go.'

'That's just the doping. There are plenty of other ways. Standover chaps threaten the jockeys. And some aren't above taking a bit on the side to lose. I believe the going rate at the moment is a hundred grand – depending on what's at stake. It buys a jockey a lot of diuretics.'

'Diuretics?'

Cameron nods. 'Passing water is a tried-and-true method for losing weight.'

I cut across him. 'Well, thanks for the ancient history, but you still haven't answered my question. How are they doing it now?'

He spreads his hands. 'That's just it. I don't know. You see, it varies. For instance, take that jockey –'

'Cyril Golightly?'

Cameron nods. 'He was a good little jockey. I'd tell him to win, and he'd win. Yet on the day of the accident, he simply – fell off his horse. We had to have the animal destroyed and, as I recall, the jockey wasn't worth much afterwards, either.' He considers me for a moment before continuing. 'Similar things have happened a few times since, but not on a regular basis, you understand. The people involved vary their – how would you put it – modus operandi.'

'So it's horses for courses?'

'If you want to put it that way, yes, it's horses for courses. All I know is that when I'm most certain of a winner something happens that makes the race turn out otherwise. I find it most – annoying. You see, Mr Black, while I don't need to win, I don't appreciate not doing so.'

I lean forward. I've got the money. All I got to do now is earn it. 'All right. Who would want to stop you winning?'

'I'd tell you if I knew, I really would.'

I nod. They like to see you nod. It makes them think there's an outside chance you believe what they're saying. 'Okay, I'll do it the hard way. Who stands to benefit if you go under? Or, another possibility: who hates you enough to want you to take a dive? And who knows, we might come up with a name that's comfortable in both camps.'

'Mr Black, again, if I knew that, I wouldn't be coming to you; I'd go straight to the police.'

'But you didn't come to me, remember? I came to you. How about telling me why someone might hate you enough and also how someone might benefit by your losing – and leave it to me to put a face on the figure.'

It's like greasing rust. However much you add to the bearings, the wheels still don't want to turn. But after a while the axle always gives up the unequal struggle and breaks.

'I really don't know.'

'Okay, last question: what gives with the track?'

'What track?'

'The faux course, the racetrack as big as Randwick, your private peccadillo.'

He shakes his big shakeroo. 'Sorry, but that's out of bounds, to you and everyone else. I had to talk to that bloody newspaper about it because it was spotted on Google Earth, until I had it unspotted. But that's irrelevant to your inquiry. This is about the death of Angela Golightly and I'm buying your services to solve that particular matter. No-one visits my track, except by invitation, even if that someone happens to be helping me out of a –'

'Fix?'

Cameron shrugs. 'Your word, not mine, Mr Black.'

I stand and hold out my paw.

'More money? But I've already –'

It's not more money I want. 'I thought a handshake would be in order.'

People like Cameron don't like getting their mitts dirty, but after a while, in a bizarre hand-over gesture, he takes my right with his left, and produces the sort of shake a dead fish would be proud of.

The speakeasy looks like a bomb hit it. Tables are upended, there are broken bottles, and Hank the barman's wrestling with the nickelodeon, which is reclining on its side by the GENTS.

'Where's Cyril?'

Hank shrugs the straps of his pink singlet back on his waxed shoulders and straightens. 'With any luck, the little beast has gone to the Devil and taken his stupid toy with him.'

I could ask what happened, or I could help Hank pick up his music box. I help with the music box. Hank's wearing Chanel Number 9 and a cross expression on his dial-up.

'Here's fifty, look after Cyril for a moment, there's a good lad.' A curl breaks free as he shakes his head. He tucks it back into place along with the others. 'Christ, Rainbow, you may as well have asked me to babysit a wild bull.'

A wild bull? Cyril?

Hank heads behind the bar where he finds a broom and starts in on a round of sweeping. 'That boyfriend of yours is severely manic depressive – and you left me holding the manic part. He had too much to drink and after that he wanted to bet on – well, anything, really. He wanted to bet on who'd walk through the door next, and when no-one would bet on that –'

'He just lost someone close to him.'

Hank exchanges the broom for a long-handled cleaning scoop. 'Rain, everyone loses someone close to them, but they don't go around creating mayhem over it.' He shoves bits of broken glass in a garbage bin and slams down the lid. 'You know what he did when no-one would take his bet? He called them a bunch of wankers. So Hair-Trigger Hoffman – who'd just walked through the door – started breaking bottles – which happened to include a 2005 Grange that was just there for show. Then Harry the Wolf upended some furniture. Crazy Jane interceded and that's when the cops showed up.'

I slip Hank a couple of the crisp green bills Cameron gave me, after which I palm him another couple. Grange doesn't come cheap, not to mention hurt feelings.

'On the bright side,' I say, 'it looks like all the baddies have gone home.'

Hank tucks the money into his jockstrap. 'Everyone except Cyril.'

I glance around. 'You kept hold of him?' I palm Hank another C-note. 'What happened to him?'

'The cops tasered him. He's in one of the cubicles.'

Sure enough, Hop-along's locked in a stall, still hugging his horse. I push his head into the bowl and press flush.

'Wha-wha?'

'Wake up, mate, we got work to do.'

At the serried-eyed time of eventide, Kings Cross is like a madman with the pills wearing off – quiet for the moment, but you know what's ahead so you quickly get yourself elsewhere. And I know where that elsewhere is. Money or no money, Justin Cameron's still suspect number one.

'You used to ride for Cameron,' I say to Cyril. 'Therefore you'd know the location of his racecourse.'

Sometimes people are stupid and sometimes they just play stupid. 'Wha – what racecourse?'

I stay on track. '*Cameron's* racecourse. The private track where he trains his string of thoroughbreds.

The track he had built along the exact same lines as Randwick.'

Cyril's collar is torn, what hair he's got left looks like the rats have been at it, and his toy horse looks like it's gone ten rounds with a crazed orangutan.

'She's gone.'

'I know she's gone.'

'Iss all right for you.'

I drag Cyril to his feet and the rest of his collar comes off in my hands.

'Listen, you' – with difficulty I avoid the obvious epithet – 'it's not all right for me, got it? It's not all right for anyone except the bastard that killed her. It's –' I pause in the peroration. Cyril didn't do anything deliberate. 'Okay, it's not all right for you, either. But the difference between you and the rest of the world is that you get drunk and depressed while the rest of the world –'

But he's stopped listening, so I feed him something to start him again. 'Where's Cameron's track?'

He gives me one of his funny looks. It tells me that while he knows where Cameron's track is, he also knows something else.

Chapter 21

THE DARK HORSE

We find Annie near Central station again. Gertrude's all booted-up and Annie's leaning over the usual dirty figure huddled under the usual dirty blanket.

'Hi Annie, any more unexplained corpses?'

She straightens. 'Nice to see you again, Rain.'

'Cyril, this is Annie, she helps people.' I note her practised eye take in the shambling wreck by my side. 'Annie, this is Cyril, he used to be a jockey but now he's a useless gambler.'

'Hi Cyril.' Annie nods briefly in Cyril's direction before turning back to me, her face soft in the moonlight. 'Yeah, there's been another since – since last time …' She shakes her head. 'Same sort of thing – bruises, scratches, tiny burns, other marks not consistent with – you know. Anyway, I told the police, but they weren't all that interested.'

'Male?'

'Yep.'

'Where'd you find him?'

'Behind those cars.'

I keep my voice casual. 'Blanket over the corpse?'

She shakes her head. 'Not even nearby.' She hugs herself. 'What do the marks mean?'

I glance at the cars Annie indicated – they're a thrown crow from the station entrance – then back at the slight figure before me. 'More than they should and less than I'd like them to. You been checking the pockets?' She shakes her head. 'Okay, if you get the chance, check 'em. Meanwhile, I got a few things on my plate right now. Maybe afterwards, I – you know, we …'

She huddles herself. 'How's Immo doing?'

I met Annie a few years back while disarming an identity-stealing gang preying on the destitute. After that we hooked up now and again, and now and again she babysat Imogene while I was out on a case. These days she's a friend in need, always there when anyone needs her.

'She's – fine.' It'll be light in a couple of hours. After that it'll be too late to do what me and Cyril have got to do. 'You ever come across the Grundy organisation in your travels?'

Annie nods, briefly. 'They do good work. People have said …'

'What do you say?'

'They do good work. They stop people gambling.'

'Do you know the dame in charge, one Paris Witherspoon?'

Annie nods again. 'Yeah, she's beautiful.' Suspicion clouds her eyes. 'Why, have you met her?'

I shrug. 'I came across her in the line of business, and like you say –'

Annie frowns. 'Just make sure you just keep your line of business businesslike, Rain.'

As we head along the concourse towards platform 13, Cyril wavers between mournfulness and mourning. 'I'm sorry about the bar, but the bastards wouldn't bet with me. I told them they were being un-Australian but that just made things worse.'

'Where did you say this racetrack is?'

He tells me where the track is and I check arrivals and departures.

'We'll just make it.' I hustle him along. 'Mate, there are other things in life besides gambling, you know.'

The little man hobbling along the platform beside me shakes his head, and the bug-eyed horse he's carrying shakes its head along with him. 'Not for me there isn't. Not since the accident. And now my beloved's gone, my reason for living's gone with her. Gambling's my way of coping.'

I don't want to be a death-watch beetle. Mum took herself and my sister out via a fire-wheel to infinity when I was a kid, meaning I've had enough of that kind of thing to last me a lifetime. Unlike Annie, I'm no babysitter.

'Cyril, forget gambling. And you're too long in the bo-diddly to be carting a cuddly toy everywhere, too.' The horse's head's just about off and half its tail's missing. 'You been putting so much work into hugging that thing, it's falling apart.'

But like the story Rube used to tell me about the wind trying to blow a joker's coat off, when I try to huff-and-puff these two apart, all that happens is that Cyril just hugs the mangy thing closer.

'Lord Haw-Haw's not an *it*, he's a *he*.' Cyril strokes its ears. 'Also, I've booked him in for a repair job.

He'll be all right after that.'

I shrug. 'It's a pity they can't do the same thing with humans.'

Cyril puts up a last bit of a fight before we get on the train, like he's just remembered something, and the something he's just remembered isn't pleasant. But I push him into the carriage, climb in after him, and slam the door after us both.

'Look, I got better things to do with my time than to wet nurse a thumb-sucking gambler. But it just so happens I owe a favour to Angel, and it also happens that you're part of that favour.'

He tries to get up but I pull him down.

'Hey, you're hurting me!'

'So maybe you want to be hurt. In the meantime, you're going to show me this racetrack of Cameron's, and after that I'm going to take steps to cure you.'

'Cure me of what?'

'We'll start with the gambling.'

Even as I tell Cyril that, the shadows fall all around me. The shadow of my mother killing herself. The shadow of Imogene. The shadow of Angela. And the not-so-elusive shadow that appeared on the edge of my consciousness after I saw the first corpse, the one that was flitting around just now behind Annie, which was one of the reasons I had to get away from her, the shadow which might or might not have accompanied us onto the train.

'How do I know I can trust you?' he whines.

'Don't you realise you got no choice? Your legs are stuffed, you lost your wife and you're in debt, big time. I'm your dark horse, and for my money you got nothing left but to put your last dime on me.' I gesture out at platform 13. 'What I'm saying is you can find an ex gratia copy of *The Sydney Morning Horrible* and shamble off to the nearest piece of parkland and crawl under the newspaper and die in the next heavy frost – or by the same nefarious means that the others are dying from – or you can come with me.'

'I suppose I got no choice,' he says.

'You suppose right.'

A voice over the loudspeaker tells us our train is about to fart. Public transport's shelling out several million Pelaco collars teaching their employees how to speak.

Until then, our train is about to fart.

Chapter 22

SEE HOW THEY RUN

We get out at Waterfall. There's a lot of shadows. They might be people. Then again, they might just be shadows.

'Are you sure you know what you're doing?'

I've got Cyril by the sleeve and he can keep up or he can fall behind.

'You sound like you want certainties,' I tell him. 'When are you going to learn there are no certainties in this world, apart from death?'

We've been followed from the station, and it's not by a guard wanting to fine us for fare evasion.

'Can't you slow down a bit?'

I stop and ease my hold of his sleeve. He smells of unwashed toy, desperation and mothballs.

'Do we have to do this? It's just a racecourse.'

'Listen up and listen good, because this is the first and last time I'm going to say it.' I've never liked the smell of mothballs. 'I got problems of my own I should be attending to. But first I'm going to find out who killed Angel.'

Between Annie's corpses, Cyril's debts, a man called Cameron, and the death of Angela Golightly, I'm thinking there's got to be a link. Like Rube says, there's always a link.

Cyril clutches his horse and a last straw. 'But it's a lost cause. I've lost Angela and whatever you do can never bring her back again. I'll just go on betting, I know I will.'

I take a deep breath. It's got the flavour of gumtrees and danger in it. 'We'll see about that, Cyril.'

Never Neverland isn't what I expected, but fairytales rarely are. At least the shadows have gone, and in their place is the following:

One racetrack, complete with barrier docks.

Four arc-lights.

A viewing platform.

A handful of horses, complete with jockeys.

And a familiar figure.

'So, all right, you've seen it,' Cyril says. 'Now can we go home?'

'What's eating you, mate? I know you must of rode trackwork here but that can't be enough to give you the heebies. Is it the memory of your fall?'

'What if we get caught?'

'Pal, you're already caught – in a web of your own making. And one of the objects of this exercise is to get you uncaught. So shut up and hang close and there's an outside chance you'll survive.'

As we draw nearer, I quarter the ponies lined up to race, as well as the person that looks familiar.

'Do you recognise the horses?'

'All of them.'

I hand Cyril a scratcher, as well as something to scratch on. 'So write them down – all of them.'

The breath of the night air is in my nostrils as I watch the beautiful creatures run, and I'm reminded yet again – if anyone ever needs reminding – of the sport's allure. The track bursts into a kaleidoscope of colour. The horses are coming into the first turn, tails streaming behind them because the farmer's wife hasn't lopped them off yet, the jockeys crouched low over the withers as they settle into their stride, wearing all the colours of the rainbow, and then some.

On the second turn, number three begins his run, a fine, tall bay with a white slash marking his face, nostrils flaring in the moonlight, flanks quivering, neck muscles straining, a faint sheen of sweat glistening on his neck.

'Want a bet, Rainbow?'

I tell Cyril no and the horses finish, then immediately form up again, as a familiar, aristocratic voice wafts over the night air. 'That was very nice, boys and girls. Let's see if we can replicate it, shall we?'

I get a nudge from Cyril. 'Come on, Rainbow. I'm on three this time, all right? I know the horse. He's by far the best over this distance and Jerry's up. A tenner straight – okay?'

I don't bother replying. Number two's holding as they thunder past, muscles bunched, sinews glistening, all the jockeys out of the saddle, leaning up and forward like they're floating on air.

Just like Cyril said, number three makes a dash in the final straight, coming up on the outside like it owns the race, legs flailing like an out-of-control automaton.

But it's number one that ends up winning.

Chapter 23

DEALING WITH CYRIL

We've made our way back to the station and I've made up my mind about Justin Cameron. But first I got to deal with Cyril. I glance down as he clambers gratefully back on the train.

'You all right?'

'A bit depressed but other than that …'

I find us seats in another graffiti-covered carriage.

'You can't go through your life depressed.'

'Why not?'

'Because that's not much of a life, that's why not.'

The little man shrugs. 'I remembered, watching those nags, that I'll never ride again. It was never so clear to me as it was tonight. And that's why I gamble.'

'Correction – that's why you used to gamble. Because from now on, you're not going to gamble any more.'

'Why, what are you going to do?'

'It's not what I'm going to do. It's what someone else is going to do.'

'What?'

I'm standing on Rory's front porch. Cyril's dawdling by the front gate, hugging his horse and looking furtively up and down the street.

'I said I want you to cold turkey Cyril.'

Roarer frowns. 'What do you mean, *cold turkey Cyril?*'

Rory's a killer. That was before he found religion. Now he just asks questions.

'Just like I say. People take drugs, you cold turkey them. Stop them taking drugs and they cease to feel the need. The same with drink. Well, Cyril here's a gambler. I need you to keep him off gambling until he loses the urge. I'm offering you a chance to win some of those Heavenly Credits of yours. I can also pay you real money.' I hand him a sheaf of Cameron's dough-re-you.

'Jesus, Rain.'

'Exactly. Tell Cyril he'll have to go to church if he doesn't stop gambling. Tell him you'll break his arm if he even considers a flutter. Tell him you'll kill him if he rings up a betting parlour.'

'But I don't kill any more.'

'Yeah, but Cyril doesn't know that.'

Cyril comes up behind me, looking like the wreck of the Hesperus. The bits of bush hanging off him don't do anything to soften the image. 'What doesn't Cyril know?'

'That I'm leaving you here with my mate Rory.'

Cyril sizes up the killer. 'What if I don't want to be left here with your mate Rory?'

'You haven't got a say in the matter. You're staying, and that's final.'

'But I want to get Lord Haw-Haw – fixed.'

'So get him fixed.'

'I've got to take him to the shop.'

'So take him to the shop.'

Cyril glances at Rory. 'But will he let me?'

'Of course he'll let you.' I glance at Rory. 'You okay with that, Roarer?'

'Am I okay with what?'

I stay patient. 'Will you take Cyril here to the shop where he can leave his toy horse for fixing while you're keeping him in a gambling-free environment?'

Rory raises his eyes to heaven. 'Why don't you look after him?'

'Because I'm busy.'

'So why doesn't someone else – Hey, what about that bunch that fixes gamblers? Mrs Grinder's, or whatever they are. I saw her on telly. She's –'

'It's Grundy's.'

'Yeah, them.'

I check out Cyril. He's talking to his horse. I come back to Roarer. 'Let's just say they're a last resort.'

I hand Roarer another hundred to help him to be the second-last resort.

'Hello?' Soft modulated tones, the sort you'd like to take to bed with you, full of the promises of Heaven. 'Is that you, Mr Brown?'

I don't hang up and throw away the phone. I'm Mr Brown, or Red or Yellow or Green – any colour the voice wants me to be. 'Why, who's that?'

But I know who it is. It's Cleopatra, Diana the Huntress, Elle Macpherson and Venus de Milo all rolled up into one, the answer to every man's dreams. I just want to hear her say it, with that deep-throated chuckle, the sort that –

'Why, it's Paris, of course – Paris Witherspoon.' Two beats. 'Known to all the world as Mrs Grundy.'

I try to keep my response as cool as an undertaker's storage box. 'What can I do for you?'

The answer's melodious. 'Oh, Mr Brown, as the late US president John F. Kennedy once said: *It's not what your country can do for you, it's what you can do for your country.*'

'Meaning?'

'Meaning I've got some good news for you. Could we meet somewhere?'

We can meet any place, but in the end we settle for the Mystic's, the one overlooking the Harbour.

The longer I live in this burg, the more I realise it's not all it seems. There's a chasm between the soft dreams it promises and the hard reality it ends up palming you. It's like everyone wants Sydney to be nice, and goes into denial when it's not. Headless bodies and bodyless heads. A nice little calling card that turns out to be a .45 slug in the back. People leaving buildings via the forty-fourth-storey window. Houses going up in smoke. Politicians on billionaires' row. More corpses on the mean streets with unexplained and inexplicable marks on them, which the cops do nothing about. And I'm still being followed.

Chapter 24

THE LATEST FROM PARIS

Say *Sydney* fast enough and it comes out *Sinny*. Say *Mystic* fast enough and it seems like it's *misty*, and that the clientele are here for the good of their health. I know better, but Mrs Grundy doesn't. Which is why I find her sitting under a sign saying 'Teahouse of the August Moon' surrounded by signs astrological, imagining she's where she belongs, which is probably somewhere between the Botanical Gardens and Noddy Land.

'Why, Mr Brown!'

Well, I know why, only I don't tell her that. Tell her that and she'll depart from my life forever, clutching her modesty in both beautiful hands, and screaming electric blue manslaughter.

Her greeting is followed by another. 'Sowaddayawan?' He's big and he's missing most of the digits on his paws, which is how I recognise him, despite the daisy light penguin suit – the hands, and the gap-toothed leer. Man Mountain is on parole between murders. I tell him I'll have a chai.

'Chai what?'

It could be the beginning of a riddle, only I'm not playing. 'I've just changed my mind, I'll have a bottle of water with the top on.'

The dame smiles her sweet smile. 'And for me a cup of chamomile tea, thank you.'

After writing down his life's history in longhand, the criminal leaves and the dame smiles her non-face-cracking smile. 'So how is it that you know the waiter?'

I don't have to disillusion her straight away. 'We met, socially.' All right, so the segue into another subject is clumsy. 'What's your organisation do again?'

The soft light forms an aura around her head.

'As I told you, Mr Brown, we cure gamblers. Horseracing gamblers mostly, because right now horseracing seems to have become even less predictable than usual, thereby creating a more than usual number of – victims.'

'Big organisation, is it?'

The coif stays in place as she nods. So does the nice expression. 'There are twenty-one of us in Mrs Grundy's, all women. Women who need help, in one way or another, but who also find affirmation in helping others.'

'And who pays for all this – affirmation?'

Mrs Grundy spreads her beautiful hands. 'As I've also already told you, people are very kind. Wealthy relatives pay us to look after their loved ones. As well, we receive generous donations.' She shoots a glance around the room. 'Oh, isn't this just the loveliest place?'

'It's a place.'

'The Harbour looks beautiful.'

'It's a harbour.' I do the pause. 'You had some news.'

Looking at her is like looking at the sun without wearing shades. I could do myself an injury. She's wearing a white, floppy, tight-around-the-neck number that gives the merest hint at what lies beneath. Beautiful hair tortured into a bun atop an expressionless but beautiful face. Slim neck, long as a swan's. Eyes that —

'Here's yer order then.' The thug takes his thumb out of the chamomile, dumps it on the tableau along with the Evian, and shuffles off to do harm to others.

When the dame leans forward, the piecrust edge of the table presses into her shapeless clothes, and makes a shape out of them. I look away.

'As a matter of fact, I do have some good news for you, Mr Brown. Excellent news, in fact.' She sips her chamomile, and the shape in the shapeless clothes on the other side of the piecrust table makes itself comfortable, while the tea makes her lips so shiny the reflection brings tears to my eyes.

I chuck her a napkin. 'The mouth.'

'What about the mouth?'

'You might wipe it for me.'

Paris Witherspoon wipes it for me, and I can hear the rasp of the cloth while she does the wiping. 'Is that better?'

I ignore the question. 'You had some news.'

'Oh, yes.' She sits back, which makes matters better, but it also makes them much worse. 'And the news is that I've been to see your Salina.'

Sweet Jesus. 'And?'

'And I believe I've fixed the little problem regarding your daughter.'

'That's' — I envisage the scene, then I don't envisage

the scene – 'Yeah, well, thanks for that.' It was a long shot, borne of desperation, the way most long shots are. And like most long shots, the chances always were that I was on a loser to nothing in the shooting of it.

'Don't thank me,' she says. 'Just thank your lucky stars that Salina was amenable.'

'Are you sure it was Salina?'

Paris Witherspoon nods brightly over her chamomile. 'A fine, upstanding lady with a decided manner and direct gaze?' That's one way of describing my ex. 'Yes? Well, after I explained matters to her, she said she believed that Miss Riesling and I had done the right thing in returning the child. She added that she thought that you were at best well-meaning, which is wonderful, isn't it?'

What was the name of the kid that always looked on the bright side? Pollyanna? Yeah, well, this dame makes Pollyanna look like a pessimist.

'And what did she say I was at worst?'

'Oh, we needn't go into that. What matters is she said that what was a potential disaster had turned out all right in the end.'

'She called it that?'

Pollyanna nods. 'Or words to that effect. Anyway, I just wanted to say that everything's fine on the ex-wife front.'

I hunt for an alternative subject and the words are out before I can stop them. 'You might be able to help me on another front.'

Chapter 25

AT THE GATES OF HELL

When I've finished telling Paris no more than she needs to know, she leans back on a cushion that's awash with astrology signs, her face as readable as a Patrick White novel. 'And what precisely do you want from me, Mr Brown?'

'Just a name. You look after dud punters. Well, one or more of your dud punters must have dropped a clue as to the identity of the person or persons who dudded them. Most of your clientele are horse gamblers. So who's putting the fix into the ponies, who's screwing the races? All I need is a name.'

Paris Witherspoon looks at her watch — a big dangly thing on her firm wrist — and straight after that she gets up from her cushion. A hard wind has been waiting for just this moment and her shapeless clothes cease to be shapeless. 'I'm sorry, Mr Brown, but I – have an appointment.'

I get to my feet, too. It brings us too close for comfort, but I'm not here for comfort. 'Just a name. Look, no-one's going to get hurt — at least no-one that shouldn't.'

She takes a breath so deep she could do a five-minute dive with it. 'I'm afraid the only name that comes to mind on the spur of the moment ... Do you know, Mr Brown, I've never really known what that expression means? Is it something that jockeys do, in order to make their mounts go faster?'

'You're thinking of whips, not spurs.'

'So why don't they call it the *whip* of the moment?'

'I guess that spur in this context means cusp, from the Latin *cuspis*, meaning point. But that's beside the *cuspis*; you were about to give me a name.'

Pollyanna frowns. She still looks beautiful. 'One name does keep coming up during the treatment of our clientele – you know, they keep mentioning it – but I can never make head nor tail of it.'

The huge waiter sidles up beside us. Pollyanna doesn't let it stop her talking.

'It – it sounds more like a geometrical shape than the name of a human being.' She pauses, then comes right out with it. 'The name is – Pentagon.' She reaches out and her hand's got the same feel to it as the name. 'But, please, you must promise me, Mr Brown, no hurt must come to this – Pentagon person.'

'Only if he tries to hurt me.'

After I leave the caff, I check out the Harbour. Politicians want to stick a heliport in the middle of it. That's all right for politicians. They don't live in the real world. But neither, it seems, does Mrs Grundy.

I ring Imogene on dead-man's mobile No. 3. It's almost out of credit. So am I.

'That you, sweetheart?'

'No, it's me, Salina, and I thought I told you to stop ringing.'

'Come on, Sal, she's my daughter.'

'That's why I want you to stop ringing her.'

'Didn't the dame – Mrs Grundy – explain things to you?'

'Your girlfriend, you mean? That oh-so-sweet-and-innocent beauty with the over-large mammaries and the cornflower-blue eyes? The one that's supposed to run some do-gooder organisation or other to help problem gamblers? Give me a break, Rainbow.'

Salina does the Salina pause.

'In fact, don't give me anything, because I'm no longer a willing recipient. Yes, sure, the dame, as you call her, fed me some preposterous story about your inadvertently leaving Imogene on the steps of a casino while you tried to save someone from a lifetime of depredation. But do you know something? I think she actually wanted me to disbelieve her.'

'What the hell would she want to do that for?' I ask.

'Why don't you tell me? After all, you're the one with the answers. Meanwhile, and I'm telling you this for the last time – Stop. Calling. Imogene. Otherwise the consequences, at least as far as you're concerned, will be dire.'

I detect a new note of confidence in Salina's voice, the kind of confidence a gambler gets when he finds no-one's fixing the races any more, or that your ex-wife acquires after she finds herself a new boyfriend.

'Yeah, but …'

The phone dies a sudden death. I chuck it in the Harbour, the one with all the little white triangles in it.

Work, Rube told me. *When such moments as these slam you in the face, lose yourself in work. There's always something to do, so get on and do it.*

The advice is like a spar floating on the surface of the sea after your boat's sunk, but I got no choice, so I grab it.

A look of relief lights Rory's dial-up when he opens his front door in response to my rat-a-tat-tat on the portcullis.

'I take it you've come to pick up Creepy Man. The missus was just saying –'

'You take it wrong, Roarer, because I haven't come to pick up anything – other than a new dead-man's mobile phone and some information.'

The downcast look on Roarer's face would look good on a whipped dog. 'It's just that the missus was saying –'

'Well, she was saying wrong. What do you know about a joker called Pentagon?' Rory goes to close the door but I get there first and jam my foot in it. 'Look, I'll handle Cyril, Roarer. Just give me the requisite information.'

So Roarer gives me the requisite information, looking to right and left and above and behind him as he does so. They call him Pentagon, he tells me, because that's the act he's best known for – *pentagonising* people. It's the shape that's left over after he lops off his victims' head, arms and legs and chucks what's left into the sea.

'But why does he do it?'

'Because he's not a nice person.'

'Come on, Roarer.'

'No, you come on, Rainbow. You can't mix it with people like Pentagon. He's big-scale drugs, and he protects his empire like Sir Boris at the Gates of Hell.'

'Cerberus.'

'Whatever.'

'I'm told he's also into gambling.'

Roarer frowns. 'In that case, I been out of the game too long. Because as long as I been killing, Pentagon's been drugs.' He adds a codicil. 'Meanwhile, the missus told me to tell you that we've had this Cyril of yours too long. We left his horse thing to get fixed, and now he's whining about missing it. If you don't collect him soon, she's going to chuck him onto the street.'

'All right already, you got my word. So where do I find this Pentagon?'

'On his boat.'

Chapter 26

THE BELLY OF THE BEAST

The boats are the size of tankers. They're moored where tankers are usually moored – in a bay called La Perouse just around the corner from Port Botany. La Perouse was named after the French navigator that landed on a pristine beach way back in 1788. These days it's where people park their containers and all the other corruption that attends the smuggling game, until they come up with something more permanent.

I'm dressed for the occasion: T-shirt, sneakers and jeans, with a knife in a shin-scabbard under the jeans. I exit the cab and make my way to the wharf.

'Well, if it ain't Mister Rainbow.'

He hasn't got a cup of chamomile tea in one de-fingered paw and a bottle of Evian in the other, but he's still big and he's still got trouble expressing himself, and he's still Man Mountain.

'You sure get around, Mount.'

He shrugs his mountainous shoulders. 'A little bird warned me you might be coming after a pal of mine.'

Ballet is like riding a bike, you never forget the basic pas de deux. So I do the half-step to the right – watching the man mountain shiver along its fault lines – after which I bend to the left, following up with the goose-step from Bach's *Jeun Homme et La Mort*, with me in the part of La Mort. Man Mountain loses his equilibrium so I find it for him, pointing him at the ground as he goes past, after which I back-end him into a stanchion. He staggers to his feet.

'No-one mucks with Mountain!'

But he's had one too many dim sims, too many potatoes, and too much KFC. He's a walking memorial to the fast food industry, a joker that's always said *Yes* to the eternal question: *Would you like fries with that?* He comes at me like an Intercity Express, and when I do the pas seul he ends up a train wreck, a mass of blue-singleted flesh among all the McDonald's wrappers that have preceded him. I drag his head up by the leash.

'Which boat belongs to Pentagon?'

'Go to –'

I thump him in the region of his last meal. 'Which boat?'

'That one.'

The tub could double as the *Queen Mary*. It's a four-decker carrying more funnels than an extended family of arachnids – white superstructure, mauve and black hull, sturdy scrabble-ladders. I leave Mountain trying to work out the meaning of life, find myself a rowboat that no-one's using, and start rowing.

It takes ten minutes getting through the filthy water and I'm still no closer to the *Queen Mary*'s hull. A jumbo from nearby Kingsford-Smith airport chops the sea into sandpaper as it lumbers skyward, while the joker in the singlet back on the wharf has woken up and is waving his arms about like a windmill. The thing about rowing backwards is you can't see what you're aimed at, only what's behind. And what's behind the joker semaphoring is …

Pandora's so much with me of late that she's become almost a companion animal, a slinking black panther rarely more than a death breath away. But the figure behind the pile of ropes behind the joker waving isn't Pandora. The figure detaches itself and slips behind a stanchion. When you expect to see something, you see what you expect to see. I expected to see Pandora, the dame in black that has pursued me ever since the day my mother died, so that's what I see as I plough my way away from the jetty. Only it's not black, it's blue, and it's not Pandora, it's someone else. Mountain's still waving but now he's got his mobile phone out. My sightline's momentarily obscured by a hawser attached to a buoy, and when I can see anything again, the figure's gone.

I quarter the wharf.

Nothing.

Containers, cars, tanks, cranes, ropes, but otherwise nothing. Nothing, at least, that I can put my finger on.

So I keep rowing, because there's nothing else to keep.

The boat's like the Great Wall of China, a giant, rearing behemoth of a thing rising sheer from the surface of the water, formidable above, rippling black below. I grab one of the grapple-ladders and start grappling.

If Cyril was around he'd place bets on a certainty – odds-on for Rainbow to get caught. The sisal's as thick as Roarer, two hand-grips' diameter, the thickness of Mountain's forearm. I straddle and haul, straddle and haul, straddle and – I'm halfway up when Mountain takes a pot-shot at me from the wharf. The bullet sings like Joan Sutherland off the hull by my head. It's only a .22, but even a pinprick can kill if it's going fast enough. I kick away hard, but not hard enough, and after I let go the ladder I crack my head against the *Queen Mary*'s hull.

Then I go down.

A good part of my time with Aunt Rube was spent doing swimming lessons, day after day at the Boy Charlton pool, followed by deep-sea diving off the Heads. *What about sharks!* I'd ask through teeth chattering like a machine-gun. *Deal with it,* Rube would say, and push me off the cliff. Since then, I've kept up the long Bondi swims, and as a result, I know my way around water. It doesn't make drowning any easier.

The rescue launch has got two outboards, and the guy at the tiller's got a sense of humour. He's also got a gun. 'Nice day for a dip.' The tiller-man waves his gat as another thug drags me aboard, as if to remind me he's still got it. 'What were you doing down there – solo synchronised swimming?'

He's more intent on his humour than on an exchange of worthwhile information, but after a while he settles down, and after a while longer a maintenance board's lowered and I'm hauled up onto the ship's deck. There I find a welcoming party about as welcoming as the Great Plague of London.

'So what's your story?' He's a thug and he's accompanied by other thugs.

'I fell in.'

'Yeah, and I'm the Shah of Persia. We got someone here wants to meet you.'

Chapter 27

THE SPECIALIST

The hands are a long way from gentle and the deck's the size of a Boeing runway.

'Who's the someone?'

'That's for us to know and you to be amazed at. So shut up.'

So I shut up. After being dragged along a kilometre or so of deck, I find myself on the floor of a stateroom that could double as the Banquet Hall in Versailles. It contains a table, a chair, and a big, fat bastard with a tablecloth around his neck enjoying a banquet.

He wipes a set of lips that could double as sausages. 'Who's this?'

'We fished him out of the bay, boss. Mountain told us to expect him. He said –'

'I don't care what Mountain said.' The big bloke's got a chicken leg in his greasy paw and hasn't taken his eyes off me since I was dragged in. 'You from the tax office?'

I tell him no, but the information doesn't compute.

'Mountain said he –'

'I thought I told you to shut up.' He still doesn't take his fish eyes off me. 'Don't you people ever give up?' He waves an arm at his surroundings. 'So I got some, so I'm lucky. Why should honest citizens have to pay tax on lucky?'

I try to get to my feet but I'm palmed back off them by the thugs. 'Because you're not honest and I'm not from the tax office.'

'You all say that. You expect us to tell the truth, but you lie like crazy. I've had a gutful of your single standards.'

I make the necessary correction. 'It's double standards. The tax office has *double* standards.'

The smart's wasted on my host. 'Whatever. Anything to declare, tax man, before my boys chuck you back in the drink?'

We could talk about global warming or the state of the economy, but something tells me Pentagon's not all that interested in social philosophy, so I come straight to the point. 'I'm not tax and I've got standards and they're not double. I'm a detective and I'm looking for a killer.'

Pentagon laughs so hard he breaks wind. 'You come to the right place then.'

I persevere. 'Not just any killer – someone that's in the habit of fixing races, who also torched a terrace in Camperdown, and took out a friend of mine in the process.'

'And you think it was me?'

'If your name's Pentagon, you're in the ballpark.'

He stops laughing. 'This friend of yours that ended up dead. Did he by any chance end up minus his legs, his arms and his head?'

'It wasn't a him it was a her. And no, she just ended up incinerated.'

'I don't do incinerations. Come to think of it, I don't do inquisitions, either. Which means you just ran out of time.' He nods to his goons. 'Feed him to the sharks.'

'Just one last question.'

'If it doesn't have to do with the menu – mine or the sharks' – I don't want to hear it.'

'You'll want to hear this one.'

'Okay, try me.'

'Why bother fixing races?' I nod at the stateroom around me. 'It looks like you already got enough. Why branch out into gambling?'

'Sounds like two questions to me, when you promised me just one. Which proves what I said about your standards, Mr Tax Man. But the answer to both is, yeah, sure, I enjoy a flutter – but only for my laundry. You know what that is, don't you?' He wipes his face and grins a sickly grin. 'I reckon even a moron like you can see I don't need to fix races for that.' He waves his fist. 'Take him away.'

'You're saying you gamble, and yet you don't fix races?'

'Mate, where did you come from – outer space? I don't have to bother myself with any of that.'

'So what do you bother yourself with?'

He contemplates me over a forkful of fish eggs. 'I'm a businessman in import/export – and laundry.' He smirks at his goons. 'Which means I can put dirty money on as many horses as I want in the same race, or buy up half the tickets in the two-dollar lottery, or just send my associates out to buy up every Scratchie in the newsagent's.' He lifts his mammoth shoulders and then sets them down again. 'I put in a million, and take a quarter of a million out. You might call it bad accounting. I call it natural shrinkage.'

He chucks me a glare. 'Meanwhile, you've just taken away my appetite by reminding me of the injustice of man to man.' He waves to his goons. 'Chuck the bastard overboard. Now.' He rips the napkin away from his neck, shoves his fists on the table, and heaves himself upright. 'And I'm coming out on deck to make sure you do it right.'

Chapter 28

SWIMMING WITH CONCRETE

Three of Pentagon's thugs hold me in the ankles-wrists-neck position while another one chains a lump of concrete in the shape of a cross to my leg.

'I'm religious, see?' Pentagon's standing over me. 'Besides which, a cross is the best shape, design-wise. It gives you something to tie the chain around. Plus the ends of the cross act like the flukes of an anchor – they dig themselves into the seabed, along with anything that happens to be attached.'

I estimate the sinker weighs in the vicinity of 50 kilos, just under a hundredweight in the old money, about the same as my Aunt Rube. As much as I like Rube, I don't fancy my chances at the bottom of the ocean with her strapped to my ankle.

'They'll know it was you, Pentagon.' Even from where I'm lying, held with my mug to the deck by the thugs, I can see that he's not too worried about the possibility.

'No-one of any consequence saw you arrive and no-one's going to see you go. And we're leaving, so when they discover what's left of you, we'll no longer be here. Apart from which, this isn't my style. If the sharks leave anything after they've finished with you, it'll be no more than a skeleton chained to a cross.' He places an iron-toed boot against my groin. 'You can keep all that in mind while you're busy drowning, Mr Tax Man.'

They haven't bothered pulling up the legs of my jeans and the knot they're employing is chain-over-chain on top of my trouser leg. I tense the gastrocs. Pentagon's boot presses harder against my groin like I was hoping it would, making it look natural when I bring up the leg they're working on.

'Hey, boss, every time you do that, the bastard moves. It makes it hard to tie the chain.'

'So hold him tighter.'

'We are holding him tighter.'

By the time they've finished, I'm not going anywhere but over the side.

Perhaps I am a postman.
No, I think I am a tram.
I'm feeling rather funny and I don't know what I am
But round about
And round about
And round about I go ...

This is what goes through your mind while a dead weight drags you too many fathoms into the wilderness, the poem that Aunt Rube used to murmur as she lowered me into the sea to practise escapology a la Erich Weiss – aka escapologist Harry Houdini – causing me to wonder funny things as I go down, like if Rube has ever been in love, and if so, when, with whom or what, and how.

I must ask her some time, after I get out of this.

If I get out of this.

Houdini specialised in chains. He knew how an escape artist could benefit by struggling while the tethers were being affixed, knew how to –

But round about and round about …

I've trained myself to go at least three minutes underwater, and I got maybe two and half left, as well as slightly more buoyancy than the concrete weight, which is why the weight goes first and I come afterwards, down to the depths of the bay as I struggle to pull my trouser leg up out of the tangle of chain.

I think I am a Traveller escaping from a Bear …

The trouser leg's tangled in the links and it's taking both my hands and all my concentration to get it free, working on touch alone, because the darkness of the ocean coupled with the speed of my descent makes seeing what I'm doing next to impossible.

No thumb on left hand – the handless hood saw to that – leaving me only four digits on that mitt, and two minutes and fifteen seconds on the chronometer accompanying it, to untangle the knot that was put together by a thug distracted by my attempts to deflect the iron-toed boot of Pentagon.

The knot that's over the trouser leg.

Which in turn is over the knife in the scabbard strapped to my ankle.

Houdini on chains: *A chain is only as secure as the precautions you took when the people chaining you were securing it.* More from Houdini: *Mess up the links, and you got yourself an escape route.*

Call it a chain reaction.

I got three things going for me.

One: getting Pentagon to put the boot in fouled up the chain, so that while it might have looked secure when they were done, it wasn't.

Two: the knife under the trouser leg bulked up the calf they tied it over.

And three: I want to survive.

I'm in the belly of the bay and I got less than two minutes. It's taken that long to work the leg of the jeans up. But the links are still cocked, because …

I can feel the problem now that I've dragged the trouser leg away.

The links have hooked themselves under the hilt of the knife.

Which means that what I planned to be my lifeline might turn out in the end to be my death line.

Through the waters I vaguely sense the throb of the ship's engines, but I got more important things to deal with than engines. Like holding my breath, and at the same time getting something under the chain links to lever them outwards.

The knife's out of the question.

The knife's stuck.

The knife's part of the bloody problem.

I hit the seabed, taking my weight on my elbows.

No time for any more textbooks. I'm at the bottom of Botany Bay with my options fast disappearing. I need to breathe. My hands are an all-but-dead man's, clawing into the sand, right one flailing, left one – the one minus a thumb – touching –

Sydney's seashore is a garbage tip, its continental shelf no more than a slippy-slide for detritus – plastic bottles, bags, tin cans, refrigerators, bits of cars, body parts …

Left fist closing over –

Sharks take off people's arms, legs and heads much like Pentagon does, afterwards ejecting various bits and pieces and leaving it to smaller fish to deal with the remains. The bone my hand closes over has been chewed clean. I identify it by touch as a rib, one of the lower five that isn't attached to the human sternum. Which means there's a point to it – if there's ever a point to unnecessary death.

Thirty seconds of life remaining.

I get the point of the rib under the chain link and lever with it, but my strength's ebbing. I'm using the knife hasp as a fulcrum under the bone, the point of which is under the chain, but it's – not – going – to – be – any – good …

The rib slips, biting into my shin, and slips from my hand.

I scrabble for it in the mud, find it, jiggle it until it's close to right, and get it under the twisted link again. This time I try to bring it up at more of an angle. Break a leg, they tell ballet dancers before a performance. It's meant to bring them luck.

It'd bring me luck.

It'd hurt a great deal, but it might bring me luck.

Chapter 29

DEATH WASN'T
MEANT TO BE EASY

I've got no more than twenty seconds' worth of air left in my lungs. And that's pushing it.

Time to draw up my will. Make that will power. Time to draw up my will power. *Idiot! Think, concentrate, focus.* There's nothing to leave anyone anyway. Not even anything for Imogene. But she'll make her own way, when she's old enough.

Trouble is, she's not old enough yet, nowhere near, nowhere …

With one final effort, I give it everything I've got, and then some. I'm in the roly-poly position, head down, feet up, hand heaving.

I feel the rib bend.

Then it snaps.

What's left of the rib jags into my shin like a spear. At the same time, there's a loosening of the chain. There's still hope, however slender.

Now – if – only – I – can – free – the – scabbard …

If only I –

Stuff the absence of the thumb. I'm using it as an excuse. The buckle on the scabbard won't come undone. Water's hardened up the leather. *So un-harden it, fool, make it work!* The missing thumb doesn't make it easy, but someone once said that death wasn't meant to be easy. Use your fingers, get that greasy tip of leather back through the buckle. Don't try to ease it, no time. *Push, for God's sake, push!*

Ten seconds.
Harder!
Scabbard out.
Chain links suddenly loose.
But there's still no guarantee that I'm home free.
Five seconds.
I'm out of my concrete boot, but only if I can remove the shoe. I try to toe it away, get the wrong one off, but find the shoe I need to remove has water-glued itself to the sock.
With my last failing strength, I push harder.
Shoe –
Finally –
Off.

My sight clouds and it's not just because of the murkiness of the water. A weight's been lifted, and as a result I feel light-headed. Therefore, it's logical, isn't it, that I can stay down here buried in this cushiony-cushion of the seabed, with nothing to worry about, and oblivion to comfort me.

But that's only what I think.

What I know – and know suddenly for a life-giving fact – is that my head's suddenly out of the water and I'm taking in deep lungfuls of air, air that says I'm not going to die after all, air that says that at long last I can breathe again. Even if it's air filled with diesel fumes. I tread water with my shoeless feet, taking in breath after breath of the stinking air while trying to focus.

Pentagon's boat has got a whole lot smaller, heading for the horizon, engines throbbing in syncopation with my head. My lungs are burning, yet somehow still functioning. No limbs broken. Stinging sensation in the left leg, due to the wound to the shin.

I got to get out of the water.

Don't ask me how I do it, because if you ask me I can't tell you. It's a long swim and a slow crawl down memory lane, every painful stroke dragged out of somewhere I didn't know existed. Once I smack into a slime-covered buoy, know it's a shark come to claim me, but keep on swimming anyway.

A boat rows over the top of me, like I'm nothing more than a rotten plank or floating plankton. I keep swimming right through that, too.

Half an hour, an hour, who knows? All I know is that in the time it takes for the behemoth boat to become a smoking black funnel on the horizon, I finally drag myself onto the shore.

'Jesus! What happened?'

It's the middle of the night and I'm on my knees and Roarer's standing on his doorstep. I know it's Roarer because I can only see the one leg. I also know it's him because I can hear his missus, Janet.

'Be careful, Rory! It might be someone out of your past come to get you!'

'It's all right, sweetpea.'

'What do you mean *it's all right*, honeybunch?'

'I'm okay, sweetness. It's only Rainbow.'

Pause. Then, 'He can't stay, do you hear me? That man can't possibly –'

Roarer's shrug is the shrug of a man who's lost everything he ever had, when he never had all that much in the first place, and when he talks, it's in a whisper. 'Best we go into the kitchen, mate.' His look takes in the mud and the blood as he helps me to my shoeless feet. 'It's got a washable floor.'

Chapter 30

OBJET DART

I roll up my trouser leg and take off the shin-scabbard while Roarer fetches a bowl of lukewarm water and a few rags from the sink. After that he parks himself on a stool and keeps watch on the doorway, like he's afraid the Virgin Mary might turn up.

'So how's Cyril?' I ask by way of conversation. 'Giving you much trouble?'

Roarer glances at the doorway again. 'Doesn't give me anything else. He keeps saying I can trust him, and then he tries to escape. He says the last thing on his mind is going back to gambling, all he wants is his freedom.'

I mop at the wound. 'Do you believe him, about the gambling?'

'He offered me an even-money bet that he had it beat.'

'What else?'

Roarer shrugs. 'He drinks a lot and he gets depressed even more.'

Me and Roarer have always been good at silence. Sometimes it's because we're on a job and we got to be silent, or be dead. Other times –

'Ever think something's missing, Rain?' Roarer

shakes his head. 'I thought that God and marriage would do it, only it hasn't worked out that way. I miss the old life. In fact –'

'Rory, is that man still there?' comes Janet's voice from the other room.

Roarer tries a grin only it doesn't work out that way, either, and when he raises his voice to reply to his hugs and kisses, he doesn't even sound like the old Roarer. 'Won't be long, dear.'

He lowers his voice to conspiracy level. 'In fact, if I was a betting man, I'd say I was on a loser to nothing. Most of me pension goes to the Church of the Latter Day Gooseberries, and the missus takes everything else. You know, I think I'd feel guilty going back to my chosen profession.' He shakes his head. 'Mate, what am I going to do?'

'I dunno. Meanwhile, getting back to Cyril …'

Roarer scratches his cheek, the one with the scar on it. He looks uncomfortable. 'Yeah, well, Cyril was pining for his toy horse, only the jokers that he took it to say the work's going to take longer than expected.' Scratching his face seems to have reminded him of something. 'Don't know if you noticed, but Cyril kept scratching himself. Well, it got so bad, I took him to a doctor. I thought it might be saddle sores.'

'What did the doctor do?'

'He got Cyril to pull down his strides and after that he made him lie face down on one of those bed things doctors have got. Then he put some stuff on where Cyril's been scratching and gouged around for a bit with a shiff. Finally, he said *Ah!* like he'd discovered the meaning of life, and tweezered something out of Cyril's left cheek.'

'You stayed there watching while all this was going on?'

'You told me to keep an eye on him.'

I think about that, then immediately stop. 'What was the something the doctor dug out?'

'It looked like some kind of needle.'

'A needle?'

'The doc said it might be a dart and got all serious on me. Wanted to know where it came from, see? He said he was going to the police over it.' Roarer notices the glance. 'It's all right, Rain, I told him I'd kill him if he did.'

'You what!'

'I got him out of the Yellow Pages, the advertisement said client confidentiality was assured.' I'm still staring at him. 'Look, it's okay, I didn't kill him. But he got the message. He's not going to nobody over nothing. Also I made him hand over the dart.'

'So where is it?'

Roarer climbs onto his foot and hops across the linoleum to the nicely-painted kitchen cupboards where he pulls open a drawer. After he's scratched around for a bit, he comes up with something that looks like no dart I ever seen before – a shiny, tubular projectile measuring about half an inch long, with tiny built-in fins of the same material on the tail, inverted.

'Where the hell did this come from?'

'I told you – out of Cyril's bum.'

'I mean before that.'

Roarer shrugs again. 'The doc didn't go into

details, Cyril was moaning and I just wanted to get the hell out of there. So we got the hell out of there.'

'Where is he now?'

'Who, the doc?'

'No, Cyril.'

'Roar-eee?'

'He's asleep behind locked doors and I ain't going to wake him for no-one.'

Roarer's lying. I know that because whenever he lies, he scratches the leg that isn't there and all he ends up with is splinters. My bet is he's gone and dumped Cyril on the Grundy dame.

Chapter 31

DEATH DOESN'T TAKE A HOLIDAY

It's morning, which means there's another unexplained corpse littering life's canvas in the inner city, and Little Orphan Annie's busy cleaning the brushes.

'How's it going, Annie?'

She looks up from a pile of blankets. 'These poor people …'

Annie feels things too much. She's thirty-something but looks fifty – trackie pants smeared with gunk, hair all over the joint, and her eyes tell me that she's been crying.

'Another one same as the others. With those same marks.'

'Did you check their pockets?'

She nods and produces a few crumpled scraps of paper.

'Betting receipts?'

She nods again.

'Anything else?'

The nod changes to a shake. 'It was as though the bodies had been wiped clean. I only found those' – she indicates the crumpled papers in my hand – 'because you told me to look. They were scrunched up in their pockets. They what you were expecting?'

'Only in retrospect.' I pocket the betting slips. 'Annie, you done good. You also need a holiday.'

She shakes her head and looks around at her bleak surroundings. 'Death doesn't take a holiday, Rain, so how can I?'

The dame's got red hair and a fake smile. I can handle the hair. It doesn't mean I got to like the smile.

'You're new here, aren't you?'

She touches the coif. 'I've been on other duties. So, yes, this is my first day in the office. I haven't even blogged on yet. But before I do that, perhaps you could tell me how I can help you?'

'Where's Prudence Shoehorn?'

'Do you mean Phoebe Riesling?'

'Yeah, that's the one.'

'She left.'

'What?'

'Sir, what business is it of yours?'

'I'm her cousin and was going to surprise her on her birthday.'

'Oh, I see. Well,' she whispers, 'Phoebe got – retrenched. For being a little too – over-enthusiastic.'

'How could that be a problem?' The posters in the office are still in place, and so is the lack of ambience. 'Or maybe my question should be: how can someone get over-enthusiastic in this business?'

'There's business and there's business.' The redhead

narrows her ee-whys, like she's suddenly smells a rat. 'But you haven't told me why you're really here.'

'Do you happen to know the reason why your Mrs Grundy sent me on a wild gooseberry chase, and nearly ended up getting me killed?'

'On a who? Nearly ended up getting what?'

'A joker called Pentagon nearly pentagoned me, a joker I find has got nothing to do with anything I'm interested in right now, apart from his own nefarious trade.'

'No, I don't. Now I'm really sorry, Mr-whoever-you-are, but I must blog on.'

'It's log in, lady. And don't let me stop you doing what you got to do. But while you're doing it, you might try multi-tasking and tell me where I can find your boss.'

'She's working out.'

That would explain all the curves. 'Could you tell me where your Mrs Grundy's doing this working out?'

She shakes her head. 'I'm sorry but that comes under the heading of client confidentiality.'

'But she's not a client.'

'No, but you might turn out to be.' She turns back to her computer. 'Meanwhile, I have to – sorry, what was it? – bog in.'

I position myself. 'While you're doing that, maybe you could give me an answer to another question.'

The dame doesn't look up, because she's busy reading from a sheet of paper on the tableau beside her. 'That depends on the question.'

'Where can I find Cyril Golightly?'

I can see her lips moving as she works the keys.

She keeps reading, nice and slow. And also she keeps typing, nice and slow. 'Real name?'

'That is his real name.'

It's like the guy at the internet bofferteria already knows that everyone's a fraud, so he's not going to waste anyone's time putting too much effort into his questions. 'Wadayawan?'

'You happen to have a spare ordinateur?'

He doesn't look up. 'Yeah.'

'Mind telling me which one?'

'Numero nineteen, smartarse.'

I type *mrsgrundy@etcetera* followed by the password I found out by the twenty-first century equivalent of holding an inverted tumbler against a hotel room wall while simultaneously peering through a keyhole. And after I key in *Golightly, Cyril*, there's the information that Mrs Grundy's minion was trying to protect me from.

You could call it client confidentiality.

Or you could call it enlightening.

Chapter 32

YOU DON'T SMILE
FOR PASSPORTS

Subject Cyril Golightly arrived in the care of a male, aged approximately 35 years, with one leg, who gave his name as Smith. It was noted in passing that 'Smith' suffers a number of what appear to be serious pathological problems that could manifest in ultimate harm to others, at the same time as he professed a strong belief in a Higher Being. NB re 'Smith': future client?

Assessment of Subject Golightly: Male, aged 37, slight physical build, a situation worsened by injuries to his legs, caused, we were advised, by a fall from a racehorse. Golightly possesses many of the traits of the problem gambler, including low self-esteem.

Outcome: While initially Subject Golightly refused to self-commit, he changed his mind on being advised that while undergoing treatment he would have ready access to excellent facilities. After being so advised, Subject Golightly proved more than willing.

Recommendation: Two weeks in the Yellow House.

Approved.

Committed.

I log out of *mrsgrundy@etcetera* and do the Wikipiddlier and Googlemania. Press reports prove to be the usual fluff. Dames' magazines run glossies of Paris Witherspoon, together with a fuzzy-faced bunch of what look like nurses snapped against a backdrop of bush that all but hides a long, two-storeyed, yellow-painted building, while the news blatts are more hard-edged, and even include one or two names. Mrs Grundy comes up in print just like she did in the not-so-skin-and-bones, smelling like a geranium – a bona fide Mother Teresa with her feet on the ground, head in the clouds, and her hand on her heart swearing allegiance to love and goodness towards all humankind forever.

A typical report, courtesy of that hard-edged news magazine, *Mothers Weakly*:

EXCLUSIVE

'There is so much evil in the world,' Grundy
tells this reporter, sadness etched on her beautiful brow. 'To tell the honest truth, I like to
think that we're like Florence Nightingale and
her wonderful nurses in that terrible war men
fought in the Crimea 150 years ago. That is, no
more than a group of ordinary women doing
our little bit fighting the evil that man does.'

Paris Witherspoon – or Mrs Grundy as she pre-
fers to be known – is beautiful. But at a time when

simply being beautiful is too often sufficient for
women to obtain fame and fortune, Mrs Grundy
turns out to be much more than just a pretty face.

Had she less depth and compassion, she might
have become just another Cate Blanchett or Nicole
Kidman or Julia Gillard. Granted, she possesses
cupid's-bow lips and blue eyes in a flawless complexion, but while her body would vie with that
of Elle Macpherson, her soul is that of a saint.

Mrs Grundy – the organisation – is devoted to
people who have gambling problems. Applying what
she calls a 'unique treatment regime', Paris Witherspoon has helped many hundreds of sufferers.

But, just as she successfully parries any attempt by
The Weakly to discover the location of her establishment, Paris Witherspoon also refuses to divulge
details of what – going by the testimony of families
of erstwhile gamblers – has indubitably proved
to be a highly successful cure for gambling.

When asked for the secret of her success, an
enigmatic smile spreads across her features, like
the look on the face of the Mona Lisa. 'Our recipe
for success is like that of grandmother's bread. To
reveal what it is would be to debase it. Suffice to
say, we use what I call "positive reinforcement"
and – as with grandmother's bread – it works.'

So everything in the garden's lovely. So why do I
suddenly –?

I look for the expected photo attributions.

There are none.

Which means that the photographs were supplied by Grundy's Inc. Also no address for the big, two-storeyed yellow-painted building. Repeat: *No address.*

Maybe that's why I –

I'm bailing out the boat when a dead-man's mobile in the bilge breaks the silence.

'It's me, Imogene.'

I picture the kid clutching the other end of the terror-phone, whispering, and my heart splits along its ready-made faultline. 'Nice to hear your voice, Immo. How's things?'

'I think she's serious, Daddy.'

I know what she's talking about, but I ask anyway. 'Who's she, doll? And what's she serious about?'

'Mummy. And she's serious about taking me away. She told me not to say anything but I had to. There's this man and it's like he's got her hypnotised.'

'Make sure you do the surveill, sweetheart.'

'I am doing the surveill, Daddy, but they're playing it close.'

'Then make sure you play it closer.' I look at the water seeping between the water boards, the place where the rot's set in. 'Where's she taking you?'

'She won't say. But I had to see a doctor and get a passport.' I hear the catch in the breath. 'When the passport people asked, Mummy said there was no father, and I wasn't allowed to smile. I don't like not smiling.' Another pause. 'Daddy?'

'Yeah?'

'I don't want to go. Can you talk to her?'

I think about what Salina told me, and then I don't think about what Salina told me.

'I –'

'Someone's coming down the corridor, Daddy, sorry. Bye.'

'I don't know what you're doing about it, Black, but it's still happening.' The big man that's usually got a self-satisfied smile on his dial-up looks a long way from self-satisfied today. 'If anything, I'd say the situation has worsened.'

'So just how has it worsened?'

'How far can I trust you?'

I'm uncomfortable but I got a lot to be uncomfortable about. We're back in the rich man's refuge and we've got some drinks and the chair's soft. But my kid's about to be taken away from me, the tail's still in place, and I'm still a long way from discovering who killed Angela Golightly. I shrug. 'About as far as I can trust you. But neither of us has got much choice in the matter.'

He takes one of those breaths that jokers take when they're several rungs above you on the pecking ladder, breaths that tend to terminate in a polite little shudder. 'Look, I'm a very important person. I'm not exaggerating when I say that I move in exclusive circles. Just acknowledging that I know someone like you could be a problem. I'm on the boards of a number of blue-chip companies. As such, I provide a great deal of credibility to racing.'

'Thanks for the curriculum vitae, but I'm afraid the job's taken.'

Chapter 33

THE TWIST IN THE TAIL

He perseveres. People like Justin Cameron always persevere. It's what makes them people like Justin Cameron.

'Look, granted I enjoy a flutter. Call it a perquisite of who and what I am. And if I win, one can put it down either to a deep and impenetrable knowledge of horseflesh, or the prerogative of the natural-born winner.' He leans forward in the button-down Chesterfield and the wall sconce turns the whisky in his glass to gold. 'But someone's been interfering with that winning streak, and I want to know whom.'

I guzzle my beer and don't bother wiping the scum off my face afterwards. 'Who.'

'I'm sorry?'

'It should be who not whom. The rest of the sentence is understood. What you want to know is who's doing the interfering, not whom. It's in the nominative.'

He gives me his boardroom stare, the one that's just this side of ignoring whoever happens to be at the other end of it. I dispense with the grammar lesson.

'I got a name – you needn't know from where,

but the name's Pentagon. I went to see him, but it turns out he's not the one doing the fixing. I also nearly got myself killed, but I'm not asking for danger money. The fact is I find myself up a blind alley without the benefit of a companion animal.' I fix him with one of my stares. Normally it works, but with Cameron I might as well be chucking fairy dust. 'Is there something you're not telling me, Cameron? Like the name of a person or persons that might have it in for you?'

'No. But I did receive this letter, courtesy of the club.'

He palms me a piece of paper. His name and the name of his club have been cobbled together using characters cut out of multifarious headings in newspapers. He has committed it to memory.

'It says I'm finally going to "cop" what's been coming to me for a long time during the races at Randwick today.'

I hand him back the note. 'So don't be at the races at Randwick today.'

He inspects the gold in his glass. 'The trouble with that advice is I have to be there. It's a massive promotional exercise. The day is in honour of a sheikh who's all set for a big win and as a result is going to make a sizeable donation. He will be in attendance. And apart from any other consideration, I do not bow to threats.'

'You realise the sheikh might cop it, too?'

Cameron swills down the rest of the gold then nods. 'That's a risk I'm prepared to take.'

'Then it looks like it might be a sheikh-down to me.'

He stares at me over his empty glass. 'Was that meant to be a joke, Mr Black? Because if it was, it was in extremely poor taste.'

I shrug. *'I'm* in extremely poor taste, Cameron. But I thought we'd already established that fact.'

The news-vendor relieves me of a ten-pointer and I take possession of the latest copy of the rag they put out with the day's races in them. It gives all the names of all the jockeys in all the races and I got a handful of them, courtesy of the list Cyril jotted down at Cameron's racetrack. I also got the jockeys' colours, and the number of horses in the relevant race. It's race five at Randwick which kicks off at four o'clock. Hard surface. I check the time now. It's two-thirty. That means I got just ninety minuets. Take away thirty-five for the taxi ride to the racecourse, and that leaves –

Four rings on dead-man's mobile No. 9. It's Cyril.

'Is that you, Mister Rainbow?'

The voice sounds weak, like its possessor thought he'd just gone through Hell, only to discover that's he's not even crossed the Acheron yet.

'You okay?'

'Far from it.'

I've worked out why, but I ask anyway.

'I think you already know why.'

'Yeah, but I need a confirm.'

While the precious seconds tick away, he gives me a confirm. And the confirm is that he doesn't like the way the Grundy organisation's treating him.

I'm back at Central, the place where they're finding the bodies, the place where all the clues are, a metropolis within a metropolis. There's a big clock in the concourse dangling low over the passing populace like the blade swinging lower and lower over the joker in the pit in that story by Edgar Allan Poe. Weary backpackers, innocent greybeards, drunks, druggies, policemen, and –

I turn my attention back to the phone.

'They started in the normal way.'

'Who started in what normal way?'

'The Brady Bunch. The Grundy Mob. You know, like Alcoholics Anonymous or Weight Busters, where everyone sits around on plastic chairs and admits what terrible people they've been to their friends and family, and after that take vows never to do what they were doing again, and later they keep the rest of the sinners informed of their progress.'

'Like they haven't had a bottle of Glenfiddich or a McDonald's burger for a week, kind of thing?'

'Kind of thing. Except this is to do with gambling, not eating or drinking.'

I clock her. It's the same dame and she's paying a lot more attention to the arrivals screen than is necessary. It's as though there's something beyond the names and numbers that she's having difficulty seeing – like my reflection. She's wearing a figure-hugging orange T-shirt and red jeans and she looks like she knows how to handle herself, standing on the balls of her sneaker-clad feet like she's –

Our eyes meet and immediately she starts moving away, a lithe figure walking slow, then hurrying, mixing it with the other shadows under the clock, while all the time angling her way towards the escalators.

Chapter 34

FOLLOWING THE FOLLOWER

I switch my peepers to departures. In the reflective perspex I can see her departing, snatching the odd glance in my direction over her shoulder, slowing, gathering speed, then slowing again.

'Just one more question, Cyril,' I say into the phone. 'You met a dame called Phoebe Riesling?'

'Her!'

'Yeah, her.'

'Haven't seen her since – Well, to cut a long story short, they got rid of her. At least they got rid of her out of here. That doesn't mean she mightn't still be working for them in some other capacity. Someone said she was over-enthusiastic.' Just like the dame in the orifice said. 'Look, Mister Rainbow?'

'What?'

'Can you get me out of here? And when you do, can you bring my horse with you?'

I'm still watching the dame in the leotards. 'Lord Haw-Haw?'

'What other horse is there?'

She's doubled-back and is moving again down the concourse of non-elegance. 'Maybe I can and maybe I can't.' She's stopped by the blatt seller's. 'On the off chance I can, where is it?'

'Where's what?'

'The address of the place you're at, followed by that of the horse-fixer.'

Cyril tells me he hasn't got a clue where he is, that he believes that not knowing where he is is all part of what someone's told him is a disorientation process. But he tells me the address of the joint where he left Lord Haw-Haw.

'But wait, there's more,' he gasps.

The dame in the red jeans has reached the escalators, and this time I can tell by her movements that she's not going to come back. I start after her, leaping a drunk sleeping it off under the clock and an old woman eating a mango by the coffee vendor's, heading for what I last saw of the dame, a red derriere making itself scarce.

'So tell me.'

But Cyril doesn't tell me. Instead there's a muffled cry, followed by a scuffle and a click and the line goes dead.

I park the phone, jam on the fedora, rebuckle the shoulder holster, and hurtle down the escalator after the dame in the red jeans.

I do the sidle-shift and the hip-swivel and the half-sidestep as I make the descent, taking care not to dislodge anyone off their travelling shoes, at the same time as I'm keeping an eye on the dame. There's no uncertainty about her progress. She knows where she's going and I like it that way because I want to know where she's going. We're out in the street. You can't assume the person you're tailing isn't going to suddenly stop and turn-turtle you, so I keep a block behind her.

I'm too close to the finish to risk blowing it now, hugging the terrace-line, ducking into doorways, keeping as low a profile as a six-foot-something private detective can keep, going into a crouch whenever she does the sudden stop-and-turn, and coming out of it as soon as she starts moving again.

She's perched on the corner of Horowitz and Cranberry, an egret-slim figure, long-necked and aware, legs slightly apart, one foot poised on tippy-toe, head up like she's sniffing out all the possibilities before making the turn.

Suddenly, she's gone. There's a bunch of buildings on one side, while on the other there's nothing but parkland. I do the pause. It's hot and the sweat's rolling off me in rivulets. No dame. Entwined lovers, pissing dog, pub, assorted shops, big double-doors to a warehouse. But no dame.

It's getting too close to the time I need to be leaving for Royal Randwick. Too late for public transitory to be of any use, so I make the call.

'I need a lift to Randwick Racecourse. Pick-up in twenty.' I check out the warehouse doors – they're big, no-nonsense affairs – the dame must have gone inside. Then I picture Little Orphan Annie next to her van, with her hair awry, at the other end of phone.

'Tell me where you are,' she says.

I give her the address where Cyril left the horse and also the address of the warehouse. And I add that when she gets here, to make sure she comes in careful.

After that, I close off the connecting link, shrug the gat into the easy-draw position, straighten the fedora, and go in.

You never know what you'll find when you go in, but you go in all the same. It's the nature of the beast, the way you get to the crux of a case – you make sure the equaliser's at the ready, and you go in.

Or try to. Only this time, it's not quite so easy. The warehouse doors are heavy-duty, with steel reinforcement over the original wood, and what look like vestiges of sound-padding around the edges. There's no-one in the vicinity. People sense when there's trouble. It goes back to when they lived in caves.

I stand back, drag out the gat and blam the lock. I push the doors open and the stench of sweat and Vaseline and vacant dust and darkness mingled with the stench of smouldering candles and burnt gunpowder hits my nostrils as I enter.

Chapter 35

A FLY IN THE OINTMENT

It's another one of those sub-sets of Sydney town, one that I take care not to go anywhere near in the normal course of things. Except this isn't the normal course of things. Because in the normal course of things, terror doesn't lie around every corner, Cyril isn't pleading for mercy, old warehouse doors aren't reinforced and insulated, and I don't find myself in the bowels of a torture house.

No sign of the dame in the red duds, not even the faintest echo of her.

I'm in an unfurnished entrance hall, lit only by wall candles, ten paces sideways, by four to the next set of doors. Doors that look much like the ones I just shot open, except for the lack of locks.

The radioactive indices of my chronometer tell me I got forty minutes before the race starts, twenty to find out what I came here to find out, and after that get to the racecourse, in order to prevent –

The candles waver in their sconces. I remember something of Shakespeare's that Aunt Rube drilled into me, that play where Macbeth and his missus dissed a king and as a result the dame can't sleep, just keeps rabbiting on about candles.

And all our yesterdays have lighted fools

161

The way to dusty death
But what's it mean, Rube? I asked her.

It means you got to learn from your mistakes, kid. You know, Shakespeare could have been the world's first private detective. If the playwriting thing hadn't worked out, I mean.

I shelve the gat, take hold of the handles of the doors in front of me, twist, and push them open.

'*Welcome to my parlour*, said the spider to the fly.' She's wearing figure-hugging yellow lycra – the kind they employ slave labour in Third World countries to stitch together using crap thread – her figure's so wasp-waisted not even the figure-hugging lycra can contract to it, and she's standing by a wheel with chains hanging off it. She's also holding what looks uncannily like a stock whip. 'You're aware of the quote, I imagine?'

I shrug. 'I take it you mean the one that goes: *Will you walk into my parlour? said a spider to a fly*. Lady, you just stuffed up a good quote.'

Paris Witherspoon goes for the big laugh but comes up with a twisted grimace instead. Once upon an age ago, Mrs Grundy was a beautiful dame. But that was when she was all dressed in white and everyone thought –

'You men act as though you're in control when really – It never occurred to you, did it, that I meant you to be here? Because I didn't want you to be somewhere else? That I wanted you to be aware of the tail I had on you from day one, so that when I wanted you to follow her, I could just twitch the line, and you'd be hooked.'

I splay my hands. It flexes the finger joints. After that, I shrug again. It eases the shoulder muscles. 'And did it never occur to you that I might have been aware of your reverse-tail ruse from the start?'

A glare of hate takes the place of the twisted grimace and a flick of the wrist makes the whip writhe. 'Well, there's only one fact that counts right now, and that is that I've got you at my mercy.'

That's when she touches a lever on the Wheel of Fortune and the padded doors swing shut behind me.

I quickly case the joint. Big clock on the wall in front of me. Ceiling, walls, and no doubt the floorboards, insulated against sound. Handcuffs hanging from the wall. Ropes with neck-sized running loops dangle from industrial-strength rafters, and on the opposite side of the room from the doors that have just been locked, wooden shutters cover what I assess to be a loading dock to nowhere.

I'm reading a sign on the wall that reads *A chain's only as strong as its weakest link* when the whip snakes out and my gat leaps from its shoulder holster and skids across the floor, while blood seeps from a cut that's suddenly appeared on my hand.

'Just in case you were thinking of using that symbol of male superiority men like you try to scare people with.' She flicks a brittle tongue over her lips, moves away from the post and begins circling me, her lycra-clad feet scuffling across the floorboards like lizards, the only wrinkles in her figure-clutching outfit the ones around her waist, the slightest bubbling of superfluous lycra that I park in my memory bank, along with the yellow Post-It reminder that I want to survive.

'I can't let you out of here alive, you know, Mister Rainbow.' Her voice is as soft as the sound her feet are making. 'Oh, yes, I know who you are. I had you checked out long ago.'

Just like I checked her out. I got to keep her talking. 'You go to a lot of trouble just to keep something like this going.'

'Oh, but there's more. And you know there's more, don't you? Except that you were never completely sure what that "more" was, were you? And if it hadn't been for the over-enthusiasm of our Phoebe, you would never have suspected anything at all.'

'Where is she now?'

'Surely you know that, too. Only you're not quite sure what she's up to, are you? You've worked out the where and the when but not the how, which is why you're here now. You thought you'd get the how from me, but instead you're going to get the what-for.'

'Come on, Paris, why don't you tell me who and where she is, and who or what you're protecting her from.' I wave a hand at the surrounds. 'After you do that, who knows? None of this might be necessary.'

But all I get in return is the mad laugh, too mad

for Paris Witherspoon's own good, and far too mad for mine. I circle away from her towards the clock that's telling me I got even less time than I thought I had.

The whip snakes out and I feel my throat suddenly go cold.

'That's just a little bite from my cat, a taste of things to come,' Paris says. 'You see, before I kill you I'm going to teach you not to be such a bad boy.'

'Like you've been teaching Cyril Golightly.' And then the big one. 'And just like you taught Angela.'

The whip snakes out again, a hole appears in my upper sleeve, and the coat starts to go two-tone – red blood on yellow fabric – and the smile on Paris' face widens.

'That kind of treatment does Cyril and his sort good.' She's behind me now. 'After all, they like the pain. And after his treatment, Cyril's never going to gamble again, I can assure you of that.'

Then she tries to deal with the second part of the accusation.

'You must understand that Angela was a weak sister. After I took over Cyril's debts – yes, I had to neutralise him in some way, he was getting in the way of our program – I tried to get Angela to join our organisation. But the stupid woman wouldn't, even though she had suffered along with the rest of us. Instead, she tried to warn her little man – the person who had all but destroyed her – what we were doing. And when he wouldn't listen, she contacted you.' She gives that time to sink in, but she's too late. It sank in long ago. 'Angela wasn't on the side of the real angels, you see, so really she had to go. She only had herself to blame. We sisters need to stick together to survive.'

The snick to my upper arm stings but I don't flinch. 'And I don't need to ask what's in it for you, Paris. Because other people's pain is just so much dogfeed to you.'

Another switch. She's creeping around behind me to my right side.

'Oh, yes, I get a kick out of this, don't worry about that.' Twitch of the lips as she circles, flick of the whip to my right knee, causing the skin over the patella to open like a flower. 'This place – the entire organisation, in fact – is how we get our own back on – because all men are –'

Got to keep her talking, find out –

'All men are what?'

'Just …'

The whip snakes out again, and the words come with each stroke, like they're forced to emerge by all the exertion.

'… like …'

Harsher whiplash this time, one that digs deep into my groin, a fraction of an inch to the left of my femoral artery.

'… Uncle Ronnie.'

She's in front of me now and her sweat has darkened the yellow lycra at her armpits.

On the off chance that I'm getting out of here alive, I need more information. 'You might answer one last question before you kill me, Paris. If you happen to know the answer, that is.'

Chapter 36

THE COUP DE GRASS

'You want to know what happened to Uncle Ronnie?' Her eyes well with tears. 'I tried to kill him, that's what happened to Uncle Ronnie. He'd been doing it for years, but Mother would never believe it, so I decided to – take matters into my own hands. He'd come to spend Christmas with us – his then-wife had left him, probably because she knew what he was, and he was alone this Christmas.'

She shudders, and instead of a madwoman in yellow stretch, I see the little girl she once was.

'One day when he was out, I went into his room and found a pile of – magazines. And among the magazines was some sort of anatomy book. I studied it until I knew it by heart. Then on Christmas Eve, I took Mum's red-handled paring knife to bed with me, so I'd have a nice little present all ready for Uncle Ronnie when he roamed through the house to –'

Her lips quiver. I keep my tone mild.

'But the knife was too small, wasn't it? And you were too weak. Apart from which, despite all your study of anatomy, you didn't realise how hard it would be to actually kill someone. Then, anyway.' I press for the information I'm after. 'But you managed to scare him, didn't you, and maybe even to mark him. Did you go for his face?'

She shakes her head. 'If only.' She waves the whip around. 'But I still got him – on the hand.'

I know, but I still ask. 'Which hand?'

I say it fast because I want the information while she's still in the mood to provide it.

'I got him in his right hand – diagonally across the palm.'

'At which point he went screaming into the night.'

She allows herself a smile at the thought. 'He didn't even stay for Christmas. He left a brief note, and there was blood on it. Mum was – stupefied. I didn't enlighten them as to what had happened. Maybe I should have. Maybe that would have …'

I don't let her slow down. I remember the report referring to Cyril's admission to –

'So what's with the Yellow House? And where is it?'

She smiles. 'The answer to your first question is it's my little joke. Do you know what Uncle Ronnie used to say whenever he did it? He'd say – and he'd sort of laugh when he said it – *You can yell out, but nobody's going to hear you.*' A look of triumph spreads across her dial-up. 'So when he screamed when I stabbed him, do you know what I whispered back at him?'

'Yeah, you told him words to the effect that: *You can yell out, but nobody's going to hear you.*'

She smiles to herself, no doubt seeing again the tormentor gripping his clothes with one hand while nursing the other as he fled the room.

'It always sounded as though he was saying "Yell

Ow. You can yell Ow, but nobody's going to hear you." Of course, we couldn't make head or tail of it. It was just meaningless words. Just like we couldn't make sense of what he did.' She winces, pauses, regathers herself and the whip. She takes a deep breath, and the lycra wrinkles and stretches. 'So that's what I called my healing place when I finally set it up – The Yell-Ow House. *THE YELLOW HOUSE*. Nice touch, isn't it?'

'Nice answer, too,' I tell her. 'Only it's not the answer to the question I asked. At least, not the second part.'

So she tells me where it is. Then she wishes she hadn't.

'What makes you think I'm going to wait around letting you ask questions, much less provide the answers to them?'

'Because it's been a secret for too long. Also you like to spin out the pain, don't you, Paris? It's your way of avenging yourself on the world.'

'On the man's world. So what's your question, dead man?"

'How were you doing it?'

'Doing what?'

'Well, for some reason you targeted Justin Cameron. Maybe it was because he was the tallest poppy you could find. How have you been screwing his certainties, killing his chances of winning?'

'That'd be telling.'

'So tell me.'

'I suppose I may as well, seeing you'll soon be dead, anyway.'

So she tells me. There were numerous ways, all of

them aimed at stopping the particular horse that Cameron had arranged to win. There were the usual methods – drugs, bribing jockeys, threats. And the unusual methods.

'Like tormenting me over my daughter.' Then assuring me she'd squared matters with Salina, when the reality was exactly the opposite. Which is a good part of the reason why –

'So what's your latest method?'

'We've been using snipers. We position them in a high point at the racecourse and they long-range a dart into the relevant horse at the relevant time from a distance. We've experimented with different – concoctions.' She smiles at the thought. 'Our first attempt was with Lord Haw-Haw. Because it was our first attempt, we neglected to allow for the fact that jockeys tend to rise out of their saddles when they come into the straight, and we – scored a behind. Little Cyril Golightly's behind, to be exact.' She flicks the whip. 'But still – same result: the horse lost. And with the building works going on at Royal Randwick – they're putting in a new grandstand – you could say we're at an all-time high in our endeavours.'

'Meaning?'

Paris Witherspoon's face clouds. 'Meaning I've already told you too much. He's going to get it. At last he's going to get it. And there's nothing you or anyone else can do about it.'

She draws back the whip and a sad look replaces the cloudy one.

'You know, I've rather come to like you. It's such a pity it has to end like this. I don't think you're just out for what you can get.' She takes a deep breath. 'But I can't possibly leave you alive now, can I? Not after telling you so much. We're ready for the coup de grace at the racecourse. And now I have to put you out to grass, too.'

She flicks back the whip.

'So goodbye forever and forever and forever, Mr Rainbow.'

It's a child's voice, like a kid saying goodnight to her Mum before cuddling up to her favourite toy, all soft and sleepy like she's got no control over what she's about to do next. Which in the kid's case would have been going to sleep, but in Paris Witherspoon's case it's killing me. She's got her back to the whipping-post and she's in the full-death position – legs apart, hair down, head up, eyes glinting, whip hand out. The clock on the wall tells me I got eight minutes to be out of here. That is, if I'm ever going to –

'Aren't you going to beg?' The question takes me by surprise, when it shouldn't. 'They all beg, so why don't you?'

Chapter 37

TROUBLE WITH LYCRA

'I'm past begging, Paris. From an early age, I've been in pretty much the same place as you. The difference is, I've resolved it in other ways.'

I think of the bully boys in the playground, before Aunt Rube pulled me out of school and taught me how to survive.

'I mightn't have had an Uncle Ronnie, but that doesn't mean I haven't been in dark places. So I know half the fun for the people that put you in such places is hearing you scream. As a result, I'm not going to beg; I won't give you the satisfaction.'

A look of uncertainty crosses her face. It only lasts a nanosecond, but it's enough. I see the whip hand waver. I've established a link with my tormentor. They don't like that. Nor do they like their victims turning on them, which means she's got another cause to be upset as I launch myself across the torture-chamber at her, keeping to my right, the side with the lash in it, because that's the safer option.

With the whipping-post behind her, and me crowding in on her from her left, she hasn't got room to swing a cat in. But the cat still snakes at me, Paris's cut-down cat o' nine tails. I roll myself in a tight ball, clutching my shins, head between my

172

knees, but the razor-snake snaps at my right ear – I hear the scream and the crack of it, the sting as it threatens to do to me what the knife did to Uncle Ronnie – but I'm past and behind the whipping-post as she turns.

She goes into the full crouch and I see her eyes glint and her thighs tense as I feint to the right before coming at her from the other side, hands out for a grip on something – anything to get her off-balance – and finding lycra. Lycra's a second skin that clings so tight that mostly there's nothing to get a purchase on. It's a bunch of tiny filaments that can stretch many times its length. Which means that even if I manage to get a fistful of it, it will be something like grabbing the rubber band of a slingshot.

It doesn't stop me trying.

Nothing to get a grip on now except hope, but there's not going to be a second chance, so I get my hooks into the place where the stuff's bubbling around her waist – the skein of second skin – and hang on like grim death.

There's nothing else to hang on to.

Waist not, want not.

When lycra's put together it's only as strong as its seams. And these seams are useless.

In a second, Paris Witherspoon is like a snake sloughing in a quiet corner of the bush at the start of summer, her spandex peeling open like a banana

– at the points where it's been sewn together.

There are sights men shouldn't see, and this is one of them – Paris Witherspoon, a woman of eye-glazing beauty, stripped to her bare essentials, feet apart and crouching as she circles, snarling.

There's no pretence now, because there's nothing left to pretend about.

The outer doors might be shot out, but the inner doors are snapped-to and my gun's on the floor by the escape hatch and there's no way I can go for the knife. So I keep my eyes on the whip and my body in tandem with Paris' – a pas deluxe to the death – her and my legs apart like his-and-her towels. We're both in the full-crouch position, arms out from our sides, moving as though an invisible cord links our hands, feet and bodies, her past and my past, as well as both our futures.

The clock on the wall gives me three minutes, four at best.

We've done a forty-five degree turn when I go into the leap. What throws her is that she expects me to leap at her. Instead, I hurl myself backwards, throwing myself into a handstand and arching my back like the acrobat in *Les Sylphides*, and holding it just long enough for Paris to think she's won. That's when she drops the whip and comes for me, teeth bared, fingers clawing the air. Hate's good in an opponent. It gets in the way of their judgment.

Bending my elbows, I launch myself rafter-wards.

Fear and anger have got the better of her. She lands sprawling, but spins as I come for her, throwing herself sideways, at the same time bringing her leg around, straight-kneed, collecting me where I never want to be collected, and I go down.

I'm on my back and she's leaning over me, snarling and clawing for my eyes, mouth, ears, hair. I grapple for her wrists but they're slippery. Nails rake my face as her hands seek for my throat. I try to break free, but suddenly and inexplicably she's too strong.

Then I realise it's not her strength but my own growing weakness. My vision starts to fade. I relax my hold. My arms weaken and fall away. I feel her fingers tighten around my throat.

I can't see the clock any longer and there's no time any more, just the blood-red vista of the ceiling of the torture chamber, Paris Witherspoon straddling me, her once-beautiful face close to mine, sucking in breath like she's drawing sustenance as my weakened fingers claw at the floorboards, and my fingers close on –

I expected nothing but dust and splinters, nothing to provide anything that might go by the name of hope. And true to my expectations, my hands close on – nothing.

I'm seconds from infinity. Death has me in her arms. Time to say my goodbyes. But I've only got one, it's all I've got breath and time for.

Goodbye – Imogene – I'm – sorry – that – I – failed – you – I –

'Die, Uncle!'

There's an injustice here. I'm nobody's uncle. My only sister's dead. My mother killed her just like this

woman's killing me now. Meantime, Imogene's alive
while I –
    I've got thirty seconds.
    After which, there's no time at all.

Chapter 38

PIPPED AT THE POST

That's when I hear the sound of splintering wood and clanging metal, and through the haze of death I see the locked and sealed doors smack inwards, and in their place –

It's not possible. I'm dying and as a result I'm seeing things.

Not angels and whipcord beauty and clouds floating in a haze of song or my past life, but a careering, drunken bull bar and attached to it the snout of an old van, a split-screen Kombi with shards of timber all over its split screen and what looks like a brand-new scar on its left cheek, and behind the wheel a white, white face and a set of fists white-knuckling the steering wheel, black eyes staring into the gloom as the bull bar comes up hard against the whipping-post, there's a terrible scream, and then everything –

Stops –

Dead.

There should be bleak blackness, emptiness. The world should have stopped. There is no life after death. So why am I hearing my heart thud and a woman's voice calling my name, as though across the echoing depths of a canyon?

'Rainbow! Answer me!'

Aunt Rube tried to get me to imagine death. It was part of her training. *See it for the nothing it is, so that you know exactly what you're avoiding. It's nothing. And if death is nothing, then it's nothing to fear, is it?*

It's nothing.

So why should there be a voice in it?

Or sirens, great, wailing, howling, caterwauling sounds, the sirens that drag sailors to a watery grave.

'Rainbow! Come on! We've got to get out of here, the police are coming!'

It's that last that does it. Eyes opening, sleepy-time eyes, eyes full of the muck of childhood blinking in the harsh light of a torch held by a torturer. To see —

The bleak interior of the torture chamber. All the necessary accoutrements — spinning-wheel, whips, chains, ropes, spikes. And a lifeless body, blood already yellowing on its beautiful crushed chest, crushed against the whipping-post by the bull bar of a Kombi called Gertrude.

Small hands under my armpits, dragging at me. My rubbery legs refusing to work, until —

'That's better.' It's the voice of a street nurse trying to raise a derelict from the dead. 'We've got you upright. Now lean on me. Just a couple more steps and you'll be in the van.'

I feel the small, determined hands under my back as Annie heaves me into Gertrude. Then the door slams shut and another door – it must be the driver's-side door – opens and closes, and the air-cooled flat four starts, followed by the familiar whine of Gertrude in reverse, a screeching stop, the grating of gears, and Annie screaming, 'Hang on!'

We've stopped once, or maybe twice, and I'm no longer in the back of the van, but on the bench-seat next to Annie, trying to remember something.

'Where is she?'

'Dead, crushed against her own whipping-post. Jesus, Rainbow, who the hell was Paris Witherspoon, anyway?'

I shake my head as I try to straighten in my seat. 'Just another one of life's little victims. Where are –?'

'Your hat and your gun? They're on the seat beside you. Meanwhile, I figured you needed to get to the racecourse.'

'How did you –?'

'At first, I thought it was just a woman's jealousy.' She hurries over that one. 'But then I realised that it might be for real, and that there could be a good reason for my dislike of Paris Witherspoon. Women get their hooks into men. But I knew her hooks were – different – and that you weren't in danger of being seduced so much as – being killed.'

'Where are the cops?'

'I threw them.'

'What do you mean you *threw them*?'

A smile from Annie, in the harsh afternoon light

the warm glow of a soft smile. 'Not in the sense you're thinking. The police pulled Gertrude over and asked what was under the blanket and I told them –'

I see Annie colour. It might be a reflection from the rear-vision, but I don't think so.

'And you told them what?'

'– that you were just another derelict.'

'And they believed you?'

She shrugs. 'They know me, they know what I do. What was there not to believe?'

Chapter 39

DON'T FRIGHTEN
THE HORSES

'You'd better clean yourself up,' Annie says. She reaches across and pulls open the glovebox. 'Use that cloth there. I'm getting you to a doctor.'

I pick up the cloth and start using it. 'Thanks, Annie. But there's no time for a doctor. We got to save Cameron.' There's dust all over the dashboard but I can see enough of the clock to worry me. 'As it is, we might be too late. You'll have to step on it.'

'We'll go to the doctor afterwards then.'

It hurts to shake my head, but I still shake it. 'No, after that, we got to save Cyril.' I glance around. 'Did you get his horse for him?'

'You forget that's what I do. I pick up things.' She jerks her head towards the rear of the van. 'Lord Haw-Haw's in the back.'

Racecourses are where the money is. They're also where the trouble's going to be. Paris warned me as much just before she clammed up for good. We're in the layby outside the main entrance. I come round to Annie's door after I climb stiffly down out of the van.

'Wait for me?'

'Sure thing, Rainbow.'

I head for the turnstiles. I've wiped off as much of the blood as I can, but blood tends to spread, and there's something about having blood on you that makes people nervous. I got my collar up and hat pulled low over my eyes but there are still the scratches on the lower part of my face, so I can't blame security for zeroing in on my potential as soon as I show up at the gates. It's becoming a familiar refrain.

'I'm sorry, sir, but I'm afraid I can't let you in looking like that.'

They're trained to be polite. *Don't frighten the horses*, they're taught at their crime-fighting academy. And before that: *Do nothing to put fear into the punters*.

'Not as afraid as you'll be if you don't.'

'And how might that be?'

I don't show him how it might be. Instead, I show him how it is. And I do that by palming him one of Cameron's hundreds. Money talks and the foe-gendarme's listening. He takes the C-note and steps back.

'I'm sorry, sir.'

It's a different kind of sorry to his first one.

I find my way to the marquee. It's big and it's full of men with money. No women, because it's men's day – men in expensive suits, sheikhs in expensive sheets. I make my way towards the big figure wearing the big smile and holding the even bigger glass of champagne.

'You'll find it to be a prime investment,' he's telling an associate.

'I need a word with you, Cameron.'

No more Mr Nice Guy. Cameron notes the change and the champagne spills and the smile's replaced by a frown. 'What are you doing here?'

'You told me to be here, remember? I'm here to save your life.' I wave my arm around the marquee. 'Not to mention the lives of your – friends.'

I hesitate on the word because people like Cameron don't have friends, just people that are afraid to say No when he invites them to the races. A knot of muscle – otherwise known as a masseter – gets to work at the edge of his mandible.

'Look, that was just a moment of uncustomary weakness.' He's had too much to drink. In fact, he's had too much of everything. 'This is a racecourse. No-one's lives are under threat here.'

'I know what you been up to, and I also know why you hired me. You got about as much probity as a sparrow. You been fixing races since the year dot. And up until recently, it was enough to slip the odd four-legger a Micky Finn or a bolter, at the same time as you paid off a couple of riders. Yeah, all those things you told me you'd never stoop to.'

The other big punters are glancing in our direction – and Cameron moves me towards the flap-doodle of the doorway.

'But things started to go wrong, didn't they?' I continue. 'Races stopped being predictable. Starting with Cyril Golightly's fall.'

Cameron's gone white under his Bay of Biscay tan. 'This is all conjecture.'

'Somewhere along the way, you got the bright idea of setting up your own private racecourse where you could rehearse races. It was your insurance policy. Why else would you use a ballet choreographer to stage manage races in advance? And it all worked nice and sweet – until your past finally caught up with you.'

'What past?' Cameron grabs my arm and half-drags me from the tent. 'Look, I have a position to maintain, while you – I could have you arrested, do you know that? I knew I made a mistake hiring you. You're supposed to be working for me, not against me. Also I'm on my homeground, which means that with just a flick of my fingers, you'd be gone.'

I shake my head. 'The reason I'm working for you, is that you preferred me' – I glance back at the marquee – 'to be in your tent piddling out rather than on the outside piddling in. You were afraid that left to my own devices, I might discover too much. Which is why you didn't want me to witness you rehearsing your races.'

'Are you threatening me?'

'No, but time is. You choreographed the fifth, remember? This is the big one, the one in which you hope to make a killing for yourself and your – investors. But it just so happens that your nemesis knows that, too, because one of her minions was following me when I paid a visit to your private racecourse. Which means it won't be your killing, but hers. Because the fifth is when she's going to make her play.'

'What nemesis? What play? What the hell are you talking about?'

I glance towards the western end of the devil's playground. A figure wearing a yellow hi-vis work shirt is lugging a black box up the outside of a platform crane, the crane they're building the new grandstand with.

'Racing used to be a matter of horses for courses, but now it's about to become horses for corpses. Because your past has just caught up with you, Mr Justin Cameron, AO.' I do the pause. 'Or should I say, Uncle Ronnie.'

Chapter 40

THE KILLER ON THE CRANE

'But that's not my name.'

'It might not be now, but it was then.'

'Wh – when?'

'We both know that you destroyed more than one life when you seduced Angela Golightly. But you had history, didn't you? Including when you used to go into a certain bedroom in the house of your trusting sister.'

That's when I grab his mitt – the right mitt, the one he avoided shaking my hand with – and twist it over. He's had plastic surgery, but the scar's gone red against a hand that's just gone as white as Cameron's aristocratic features.

'You got stabbed for it. And today you could get killed for it.'

All the confidence, all the savoir faire – not to mention all the born-to-rule arrogance – is suddenly sucked out like air out of a badly-tied party balloon.

'Is she – was she – has she been –'

'Behind your fall in fortune?' I nod. 'In between her other nefarious work, little Paris Witherspoon also found a way to fix your fixes. She waited for you to put your money on a race, then took steps to reverse your fortunes. It was a nice little version of the Chinese water torture. It didn't matter how many jockeys you paid off, or how often you rehearsed a race, she could always reverse the process.'

He looks nervously about him. 'How did – will she – is she going to –'

'Yeah, if I don't do something about it. And you know, such are my feelings towards you right now that maybe I wouldn't bother doing anything about it if other lives weren't at stake beside yours.'

I glance towards the crane. The figure in the hi-vis work shirt is more than halfway up to its deadly destination. The commentator's started his commentary on race five, telling everyone how they can win just by putting the house – and then some – on the favourite. And that's when I hightail it away from the marquee and towards the crane. The punters scatter. You're not supposed to drop betting slips on the ground, especially before a race, but that's what happens as they get out of the way.

'This is the best field we've seen at Royal Randwick for years, and we've seen some beauties, ladies and gentlemen. Flying Sheikh's the favourite, but that doesn't mean he can't be beaten. This race is wide open, without any shadow of a doubt. Let's take a look at the form.'

I belt through the masses, past the tubs of multi-coloured flowers, whitesides clattering on the tarmac. I get a foot on the first of the two hundred rungs that lead to the platform at the top of the crane.

'So let's look at today's track. Different conditions suit different horses – or as they say, it's horses for courses.'

It's a long climb and there's no longer any sign of the figure in yellow. Which means that by now the killer will be setting up on the platform after which these cranes are named. I reckon I've got a couple of minutes. But I haven't reckoned on the bird.

I'm halfway up and already tiring when the magpie makes its presence known, a black and white bundle of feathers that comes at me out of nowhere. A lot of feathers, but more beak than feathers. Magpies ought to be vegetarians, but tell that to the birds. This one likes me a lot better than is going to be good for my health, because I need both hands to cling to the crane and I'm fifty rungs above ground level, and still climbing.

'It's been hot today but the ground staff have been busy, and we've got some of the best groundstaff in the world at Royal Randwick, so —'

I let go one hand to try and bat the bird away, but that doesn't help. The voice on the Tannoy's still loud but the punters are small as the toy horses are shuffled into the barrier stalls by their even more minuscule jockeys.

The bird's still diving and swooping. Twenty rungs to go. Dizziness assails me with almost as much vigour as the bird, a wave of nausea that makes me want to let go.

Rubbish.

I snap out of the trance long enough to realise that the caller's started calling the race.

But why would he say rubbish?

That's when I remember that *Rubbish* is the name of one of the runners in race five. It's also what Rube used to say whenever it looked like I was thinking of giving up, on anything – whether it was the conjugation of an irregular verb, a ballet move, or a boxing contest.

Fifteen rungs to go.

The magpie's showing no signs of weakening in the straight. If anything, it's got more ferocious. Meanwhile, the horses far below slide easily into their second lap as my hands slide on the rungs. I'm close enough to the top to feel the movement of the crane as the sniper shifts position above me. I suddenly realise this isn't just a fix, a dart to the neck of the favourite as it enters the straight.No, this is going to be a massacre.

Five rungs.

Just like with high buildings, there's a natural sway to cranes. The sway's engineered into them. But knowing that doesn't make it any easier to hang on during the swaying, not with the handicap that Mad Maggie's providing as she does her best to dislodge me. I shake my head. It brings my blurry line-of-sight into contact with the ground, together with the gay array of colour spread out far below, and I see it through the eyes of the sniper.

By the size of the box he was carrying, I'd estimate he's got a 7.62mm M134, the kind of weapon they attached to fixed-wing gunships like the AC-47 Dakota — also known as Puff the Magic Dragon, because it's a nightmare, the kind of nightmare they used to gun down unsuspecting civilians in Afghanistan, before they perfected drones.

Chapter 41

ANOTHER FALLEN WOMAN

They're coming into the straight, calls the caller.

I hear a shot as the cabin tips. It's like I'm getting myself into the *Wooden No*. Makes a difference, one hundred and eighty pounds heaving itself onto the platform. Enough of a difference for the shooter to straighten after getting off just the one shot and swing the not-so-sweet cherry-bowl of the multifarious-muzzled machine-gun around to the threat that's coming at him from the rear.

Only the gunner isn't a him, it's a her. And it's not some random sniper picked from an orchard, but the dame that purloined my daughter from outside the punters' sweatshop, and after that graced the front desk of Mrs Grundy's, and after that – allegedly, anyway – got herself retrenched for the heretofore unacknowledged crime of being over-enthusiastic in the pursuit of her duties.

There's a look on Phoebe Riesling's face that I never want to see again, but I know I'm going to. A couple of paces. That's all there is between me and certain death – paces I can't possibly take in time – as the sun glistens in a torrid sky above, while, far below, the caller tells whoever's interested after that single shot winged its way into the marquee, that everything's going according to plan. Only it's not the plan that Cameron set in place – courtesy of a choreographer who thought he was all set to become the turf's next George Balanchine – but the plan of Cameron's nemesis, Phoebe Riesling's sister, Paris Witherspoon.

Behind Phoebe's snarl, I glimpse the features of a once-sweet girl before she was hurt – the wide-open eyes, now life-hardened; the once-cherubic mouth, now segued into a slit of fury; and the once-soft, trusting hands of a child that have turned into the talons of an avenging harridan, clawing at the controls of a primed-to-kill machine-gun.

Pity about the magpie. Because suddenly the bird realises there's something else on the platform, and that something has interposed itself between the magpie and a good feed, and the bird's just not going to stand for it.

Instead it's going to fly for it.

It's like Maggie suddenly remembers that, from a standing start, it can travel at over 30 miles per hour – that's 60 kilometres in the new money – which means that it covers the distance in one-tenth of a second, or faster than the blink of an eye.

Which is a shame for Phoebe Riesling, because she cops a beak full in the face. She utters a piercing scream and staggers back towards the edge of the platform, arms flailing and hands clawing for a handhold they're never going to find, not in this world, nor in any other.

I hurl myself towards her, reaching out in a vain attempt to save her from falling into the abyss yawning behind her.

But she flings out her arms as she goes out backwards.

For a moment she hangs as if suspended, her yellow hi-vis shirt opening like a bat's wings. It looks as though, by some miracle of engineering, she's going to beat the rap.

But it's only for a moment. Because after that, gravity wreaks its inevitable mischief and Phoebe Riesling becomes nothing more than a saffron-coloured handkerchief fluttering to the ground.

Another fallen woman.

I don't wait for her to land. I don't need to. What I need is to get off this crane as fast as I can without dying in the attempt, and before some joker blames me for the dame's demise, when the real cause was some overgrown mudlark.

I check the marquee before I leave the course. One of the trackside ambulances is in attendance, but it's not an ambulance they need. There's blood on the double-bed sheets that the sheikhs are wearing, and the silk suits of the others – but the blood's not theirs. Phoebe Riesling made her last shot count. Justin Cameron will never again be the winner he once was. In fact Cameron will never be anything he once was, because Justin Cameron AO – also known as Uncle Ronnie – has just received another honour to make up the daily double, together with the one a young girl once inscribed on the palm of his hand: a bullet to the head.

Annie glances worriedly over at me from behind the wheel of the van. 'You look terrible. Now can we go to a doctor?'

I shake my head. Lord Haw-Haw is lying on the bench seat between us. 'We got to save Cyril.'

'Where do we go?'

I tell her where Paris said it was, before she decided she wasn't going to tell me.

Night's falling as we near the target, the kind of night with too much darkness in it, when shadows cover the moon and even more shadows lurk in the shadows of the shadows.

'I'd better come with you, Rainbow.'

I hand her the gat, get out of the van, and come round to the driver's side window. 'No, stay here. There might be some deaths, and I don't want yours to be one of them.'

'Okay. But don't forget to take his security blanket.' She grabs the pony from the bench seat. 'And be careful, it's heavy.'

A creature skitters across my path as I tuck the horse under my arm and go in. An owl hoots, or maybe it's fate. Black figures multiply about me, silently shrieking. I recognise an old-style telephone booth, the kind that Superman used to change into bright-red underpants in. After that, a fence, followed by a big, yellow toilet block. No challenge. No guards, no dogs. Why should there be? This is the place where the Grundy organisation brings problem gamblers, where Paris Witherspoon and her sister – along with their horde of hell's angels – help so many mug punters beat the habit with lots of warm hugs and lollies and dancing. 'Positive reinforcement' Paris called it.

I get myself over the gate and onto a white-gravelled driveway which ends at the toilet block. Two floors of windows. Utter and complete silence. I make my way around to the back of the edifice. The doors are unpanelled and they're locked and kept that way with very big locks, while the windows are of the simple double hung variety, with sashes that slip up and down and ordinary, everyday casement catches on them.

No catch at all. And no dogs, no alarms … So why don't I –

Because I'm suddenly cautious, that's why. Something's wrong. Third window from the east end is open and inviting. Not much, not enough to be obvious, anyway. A finger's width, that's all. I reach out and then I stop dead, stepping back and ducking as I go, and a shot goes whanging over my head and thuds into the wooden ladder leaning against the wall behind me.

First round to the interloper.

I case the façade, and it's then that I see the light.

Chapter 42

THE YELLOW HOUSE

Correction: I see lights in the plural, six of them to be exact, all lined up nice and neat under the eaves on the building's northern side, each in the region of a thousand watts and pointing down at the lawn. Enough to create daylight out of darkness.

I was meant to see them, to see the opportunity and then step back from it. Because in a split second I'd be dazzled by daylight and go down in a flurry of bullets. Which is what will happen if I do what they want me to do. Which is to make a break for it.

So I don't. Instead, in one swift movement – a la Madame Blavatsky's ballet lessons – I do what I've always been told is impossible, the straight-up-in-the-air leap from the prone position, the flying fandango from a lying start rather than the demi-plié position, the ballonne into the air out of nowhere. And not away from the building but towards it, headfirst into the nearest black-faced window, broken shards of three-millimetre glass spraying out around me as the lights come on. The drought-crazed lawn is suddenly turned into a blaze of yellow ochre – just as another bullet heads my way.

I hurl myself through the window, gripping

onto the horse, arms up to cover my eyes, my body hammering onto bare floorboards on the other side. There's nothing inside the room but the broken window and a door. I take the door. I'm in a corridor. More doors leading off the corridor, light spills out from under them. And at the end, a set of stairs.

I don't know what I expected, but it wasn't this. I've only had Cyril's truncated words to go by, but if this joint is what I think it is, how come he was able to make the call? All phones would be locked and barred to the inmates. He wouldn't be able to get a message through.

That's when something stirs in my memory. Something beyond the fence. An old-fashioned red telephone box in a deserted country lane. They must have had only a light guard on Cyril because of his legs. They thought he wouldn't be a problem. He must have escaped and got himself on the other side of the gates and thence to the phone booth, from which he telephoned me, using coins left over from gambling.

During which, he was grabbed and probably –

But there's no probably about it, I know what happened for a fact as I race up the corridor, the sound of multifarious footsteps crashing behind me.

If you knew what was going to happen in life, you wouldn't do it. And if I'd known what was going to happen to me in the Yellow House, I might have fled in the opposite direction. But I'm here now, standing outside one of the doors with light spilling from under it. And when I tuck Cyril's horse under my arm and open the door, I'm back in the casino.

The joint might be a lot smaller, but it's still a casino, a shrunken version of the one I rescued Cyril from — with roulette wheels, chocolate wheels, chemin-de-fer tableaus, poker chips in teetering towers on green baize, rows of pokies, and probably far too much oxygen in the air-conditioning. Plus the players. Plus the smell. The cameras are dotted all over the ceiling, their lenses probing the collective agony like machine-guns. I zero-in on a player, a hulking bloke perched in front of a one-armed bandit bearing the graphic of an underdressed lady and the promise: *Win and I'm Yours*.

Up Yours, more like, going by the spasms in the punter's body accompanying the crazy music spinning out of the machine as the win spills into his lap — spasms so prolonged and severe that his eyes start out of his head and his limbs twist as he grips on like grim death while a series of strangled screams issues from his gaping mouth.

Ha-ha-ha, chants the underdressed lady, while a dame with a tray leans over and offers the shuddering punter another drink as he collapses, twitching, onto the floor.

I get the hell away and find myself at a table at which another dame is doling out cards to a group that consists of a geezer in a wheelchair, a fresh-faced bloke with a crew-cut, a fat man in grubby shorts and grubbier T-shirt, a skeletal joker with something wrong with his head, and a snowy-haired youth in the final stages of early-onset dementia.

The cards go flying as the fat man leaps to his feet, revealing wires leading from his forearms to the connection under the green-baize table as he cries out – his face contorted in a mixture of joy and fear. 'I've won! I've won! I've won!'

The next second he's writhing on the floor, his mouth forming a rictus and his fingers clawing the air, while the heels of his Nikes hammer the parquet.

'I've won! I've won! I've won!' he screams again. Closely followed by, 'No! No! No!'

'Yes, yes, yes,' murmurs the croupier, still smiling as she scoops together the scattered cards.

And, 'Yes! Yes! Yes!' chant the other players.

'You won! Don't you see? You got what you wanted, but it means you have to pay!'

Then, *'Play means pain!'*

'Bet and bleed!'

'Gambles means shambles.'

'You really ought to stop gambling, you know.'

The punters look at each other as though programmed to do just that, as though waiting for their cue. *'In fact, we all should!'*

I'm no Einstein, but it doesn't take an Einstein to get the picture. This is yet another place of torture, where the usual drawn-out agony of a gambler's life is concentrated in a few terrible seconds at the moment of winning, so there can be no doubt in his or anyone else's mind regarding the association.

Gambling equals pain.

Pain equals gambling.

And stopping gambling means release.

As long as the release comes soon enough.

Which it wouldn't if one of the players – correction: one of the Grundy bunch's employees, namely Phoebe Riesling – was over-enthusiastic in the performance of her duties. Positive reinforcement be damned. This is a place of pain, a sado-masochist's paradise, a torturer's hell hole. It's like the players are drugged. When they're not writhing on the floor, they're sitting at the tables and pokies pressing buttons like they're automatons. There's no drugs involved, there's no need for any. Yet another scream rends the air as yet another punter hits the jackpot, at the same time copping several hundred volts of electrically-induced pain to the more sensitive parts of his anatomy. And all the while the cameras whirr.

No-one's come for me yet.

Why hasn't anyone come for me yet? Because I'm only a threat as long as they don't know where I am and don't know what I'm doing and don't know what I'm seeing. But they *do* know all that. Because they can see me, the cameras are making certain of that, their pigs' snouts following my every move.

Chapter 43

THE WOMEN IN RED

I saw it when I first arrived at the joint, a room perched on top of the Yellow House, much like the watchtower in a jail. It would have been from there that they saw Cyril escape and went after him. And I'm guessing it's from there that they watch the pain of their victims, via the CCTV cameras. I've got to find Cyril and get him out of here. Maybe he's already dead and dumped on the street, put there by somebody's over-enthusiasm. But if he's not, I've got to find him. I've got to do it for Angela Golightly, but I've also got to do it for Cyril.

Too many players, too much action, too much in the way of distraction. Then suddenly there he is. He's won and is lying unconscious, with wires strapped to his arms under a green-baize table, still as still. Apart from the built-up footwear, he's wearing the usual gambler's rig of egg-stained bowl-of-fruit and a stupid expression on his face.

I bend down. 'Come on, mate, get up.'

Eyelids flutter. Then, 'Did – you – bring – my – horse?'

I hand him Lord Haw-Haw. I'm happy to be rid of it. It's too heavy. Christ knows how Cyril manages to lug it around.

'Cyril!'

He doesn't move. I try to extract the horse but it's already welded back into place, all freshly stitched together, and somehow bulkier, the hooves awry and the glass eyes staring accusingly at me like I'm some kind of interloper. I shake him but it's no good. He's a lift-and-carry job. I yank the wires off him and hurl them aside and after that I haul Cyril across my shoulders and get us the hell out of there.

Correction.

Try to get us the hell out of there.

There are six of them and they're all wearing tight, scarlet-coloured body-stockings with hoods. None of them is armed, apart from the protective machinery that some god dealt them – bare hands and bare feet, accompanied by the ability and desire to hurt people, employing nothing more than those self-same bare feet and hands. They're moving in unison, and with all the delicacy of wildcats.

I've got Cyril to the top of the stairs while the six dames in red are still at the bottom. That means we got the height advantage, but even from where I'm standing, I can see it's not enough.

They start up the stairs towards us. The horse with Cyril attached whangs me on the back of the head as I swing away. Then I feint, making as if to dive down towards the women. It's enough to make them hesitate – six right legs poised in the air in perfect unison. The door's behind me and to my left. Somehow, I heft Cyril over my shoulder like I'm about to chuck him, and obtain the immediate satisfaction of seeing the six-pack below me hit Pause.

But the satisfaction's only momentary. Because the Barbarellas start like gazelles up towards me, snarling and flailing as one. I'm not about to wait to see what happens when they arrive. I spin, with Cyril and his horse still over my shoulder, and my whitesides hammer the floorboards as I make for the door at the end of the hall.

I kick it shut behind us. Through the window at the far end of the room, the outside lights have turned night into day. I dump my load and grab the nearest piece of furniture – a single steel bed – and jam it under the door knob.

Chapter 44

THE FACE AT THE WINDOW

Cyril reaches for his horse – as if to reassure himself it's still there – and after that, relaxes again.

'Cyril!'

He opens his eyes and for a moment it's as if he can't see, his eyes blinking in the harsh light, sight wavering. 'Where are we?'

'We're in trouble.'

'What kind of trouble?'

'The kind that people don't usually get out of.'

The women in red must have realised the door's impregnable. I can hear them outside now, in the garden. They're not trying to keep quiet.

'You know this joint, Cyril. Is there any way out? Other than the obvious?'

Cyril tucks his horse under one arm and shakes his head. 'I've known more than one victim to exit via the window, because instant death was preferable to what he was experiencing here.'

'Okay, I thought at first we might make a drop rope out of the cordage, but now that they're down in the garden, it's no longer an option.'

A hard look replaces the calm in Cyril's eyes. 'I been here only a short while but it seems like a lifetime. They just love torturing men. They got all these screens in their viewing room. They forced me to watch. And all the time, you know what they were doing?'

I know what they were doing, but I let him tell me anyway.

'They were laughing. It didn't matter that none of us had hurt them. All right, maybe as gamblers we *had* hurt people, but ...' He shakes his head like he wants to clear it of memories he'd rather not have. 'The greater the pain, the more they laughed. Mrs Grundy was here a lot. Part of the treatment was for her to lecture us on how the various women that worked here had been hurt by men. You could see ... But there must have been a better answer than ...'

'They had a lot to laugh about, Cyril. Once upon a time they were the victims. At last they were able to get their own back.' I can hear the scrape of something hard on gravel down below. I keep talking to distract Cyril. 'They were enjoying themselves and at the same time they were curing people. They got kicks out of witnessing pain, but all the time they were spitting out punters that were never going to gamble again.'

Cyril nods sadly. 'The trouble was too much enthusiasm, wasn't it? And a few too many corpses.'

It's like death row. We're sitting together – our backs to the wall – me, Cyril and the horse.

'But why didn't some survivors talk when they came out?' Cyril murmurs.

'Would you? I mean, if you survived? It's like the women that were hurt. They don't want to testify, they just want to forget. Do people that come out of loony bins talk? Or crooks that are released from lock-up? Or soldiers that return from war? All you want to do is forget.' I remember the corpses. 'Apart from which, they didn't want to end up dead.'

It's a conversation stopper, and consequently the conversation stops. There's enough silence in the room to hear the ladder slap against the wall. I keep my eyes on Cyril. I got to keep him talking, keep his mind off what's happening outside, and of the fate worse than death that's awaiting both of us.

'What did they do to you, mate?'

He shrugs, taking a firmer hold on Lord Haw-Haw as he does so. 'What didn't they do? They might have cured me of gambling, but they almost killed me in the process.'

The silence that follows is no silence at all. I look past Cyril at the window.

He sees me looking. 'They're coming for us, aren't they?'

I'm too deep in an imaginary dialogue with Rube to notice that Cyril's been edging his way towards the window, his horse under his arm.

'It was them, wasn't it?' he asks.

'Them what?'

He nods towards the window. 'That killed Angel. My fault, but these women lit the fire that killed her.'

I don't answer. I don't have to. Cyril knows. And he's not wired like me. But neither is the horse. I know this because in the harsh light from outside, after Cyril wrenches its head off, I see red and black wires sprouting from its neck. And beyond the wires, at the very heart of the toy horse, a red light is flashing.

The horse was fixed all right.

I jump to my feet. The first dame's at the window. But Cyril's waving what's left of his horse at me.

'Back off!'

'What the hell do you think you're doing, Cyril!'

He spins on one of his crippled heels so that he's facing the dame at the window and when he speaks, his voice is muffled because he's turned away from me, the horse headless in his arms.

Chapter 45

THE LOADED HORSE

The woman is balanced on the sill and I can see two more behind her. The horse's head is lolling on the floor, but I'm not looking at its head, I'm looking at its neck, where the red light's flashing with increasing intensity like a small, naked heart. Cyril thrusts it towards the window, and the women stay stock-still, as if they know.

'They killed the love of my life. Angela died because I gambled. But in the end they were the ones who killed her.' Pause. 'Only it all started with me, didn't it? I know you're behind me, Rainbow, but it's too late. Lord Haw-Haw's already left the barrier. This is one bet I'm going to make a killing on.'

'What would Angel say if she was here?' It's a last, desperate throw of the dice, and when the cubes rattle hollowly on the floorboards, it's little more than the faint echoes of futility.

'You know, in all the time I gambled, I never once asked myself what Angela would say. Oh, sure, at the back of my mind, I had the gambler's fantasy that one day I'd land the big one and Angela would be so proud of me ...'

I take a step forward.

Cyril reaches up with his spare hand and presses something inside Lord Haw-Haw's body, and the flashing light fuses into a constant crimson glow.

I take a step back. 'Mate, it'll kill you.' I can't think of anything else to say. The women are almost in.

Cyril smiles. It's the first time I've ever seen him smile.

'Not as much as it'll kill them.'

Somehow I imagined that he'd throw it.

Instead, clutching Lord Haw-Haw to his pigeon chest, he turns to the window, takes one short step backwards and, with a speed I wouldn't have thought him capable of, hurls himself slap-bang into the arms of his erstwhile tormenters. I do a last-ditch dive behind the steel bed propped against the door.

The blast rocks the Yellow House like a ten-megaton bomb, a massive red, orange and yellow aurora of light eclipsing all else. The building's outside wall collapses in a shower of masonry, the floor turns into a slippy-side, and I find myself clutching the Wheel of Death to stop myself falling.

It's a while before the smoke clears, and when it does, the cloud cover's taken a powder and the sky's full of stars, saying *Star light, star bright* to no-one in particular. The bomb's only taken out this side of the building. From down below me on the other side – as though from a great distance – I hear a hubbub emanating from the casino room. I grab the length of half-inch, soft matt polyester 16-plait sheath rope enclosing a hawser-laid core of high-tenacity polyester filaments lying beside me, single-hitch it to the whipping-post, and ease myself into the void.

There's not much illumination, and I've got to be grateful for small mercies as I make my way as fast as I can out of this hell hole towards where the rescue vehicle should be, the one with the multi-coloured writing and the flowers on it. It is. The starlight enables me to read the writing on the side. I note with approval the added apostrophe.

'Are you all right?'

I climb in beside Annie, slamming the door on the approaching sirens. 'As right as I'll ever be. One more stop. You know where. And don't spare the horses.'

Chapter 46

THE END OF THE LINE

It's a long drive, but I owe Annie a long explanation.

'In the beginning, it was a story about an evil man called Cameron. But in the end, it was about the victims of people like Cameron, and their victims.'

Annie nods but keeps her eyes on the road. 'And their victims' victims. It's called the vicious cycle. And it started with Cameron's niece, Phoebe Riesling – née Witherspoon.'

'Exactly. Phoebe was the real victim of Uncle Ronnie, which was why she got so enthusiastic when torturing the Grundy clientele – so enthusiastic, in fact, that she ended up killing a few of them. Big sister Paris might have cut Cameron's hand, but Phoebe was the one he was molesting – the girl that had to change her name, which was why the internet history on her was as short as Cyril's legs.'

The night sky does battle with the headlights of the passing traffic. Suddenly, it seems there are no answers at all.

'So the two Witherspoon girls – and others like them that they recruited – went bad, too. There was good reason for how they felt, but they had no right to do what they ended up doing. They decided to get back, not only at the uncle, but at all mankind.

'At first it took a benign form. Paris was the brains – she tried to screw her uncle's pitch by staying one step ahead on the fixing front. I twigged to that early on, but didn't do anything about it because no-one else was getting hurt, except for Cameron. Or so I thought.'

'What do you mean?'

'Cameron was fixing races, only to find that someone was busy *unfixing* them. And that someone was Paris. Which was fine by me – she was simply fixing the fixer. But she went a lot further than that. Her front was the business focused on curing gamblers. For a while that was benign, too. She and her girlfriends had fun torturing people under the guise of curing them.'

'But then something happened, didn't it?'

'Yeah. Phoebe started going too far and as a result the clients began dying. And when they did, the protective sister dumped them in a way she thought no-one would notice.'

'Except that you knew there was something about those bodies – something different – which was why you told me to check the pockets, because you had a fair idea what I'd find. But somebody noticed you noticing.'

'That's right. And I also noticed the noticer.' I shift in my seat. 'But I was too long realising the obvious – that I was *meant* to notice her. She wore leopardskin leotards, for God's sake – of course I was meant to notice her.'

Annie picks up the story. 'Because one day Paris knew she'd want to lead you to where she'd be waiting.'

'Yeah, I was onto her, and she realised it. That was when she decided to kill me. She also decided to enjoy herself while she was at it.'

Annie shudders. 'So instead of sitting beside me, you could have been a corpse in the back of the van, after all ...'

'That was the intention.'

I try to continue the conversation, but I'm distracted by what lies ahead. Because it doesn't matter how fast Annie drives, we're still not going to make it. I know this in the same way a mug punter knows, even as he places his losing bet, that he's about to do his dough.

The joint's shrouded in darkness. Three wheelie bins stand outside, all of them overflowing. There are fast-food cartons, plastic cups, a broken recorder, an exercise book. I'll go through everything later but there won't be any surprises. Of this I'm sure. I'm also sure of something else: Salina's finally done what she's been threatening to do all along.

This is the big one, not just another simple abscond-and-you'll-learn-to-treat-me-better-as-a-result manoeuvre, but the torch-to-the-guts job accompanied by the battery applied to the private parts, a disappearing act to rival any torture that any of life's victims can inflict on any other victim in this world.

It's a variant of the oldest gamble of all – the pea-and-thimble trick. In the trick, the conjuror has three thimbles on his upturned cardboard carton, and the punter has just one chance in three to find which thimble covers the pea. Usually the punter's got a five-spot riding on it. But I've got more than that, a lot more. Because somewhere out there is Salina, and she's got the thimble. And under that thimble is Imogene.

Also in the series

978-1-922057-20-4 (digital)
978-1-922057-45-7 (print)

Winner of silver in the 2012 Independent Publishers Awards.

She's a surgeon, she's beautiful and she desperately wants
Mister Rainbow to shed some light on her husband's past.
But when he does, she wishes he hadn't. Because what Rainbow
discovers is a handless hood – and a whole lot of murders.

Rainbow's a retro private eye who keeps himself to himself.
He lives (illegally) on a boat in Sydney Harbour, has no identity,
and frequents speakeasies. He's also got a nemesis called Pandora …

The Case of the Hood With No Hands is the first novel in the
sensational Mister Rainbow heptalogy.

Also in the series

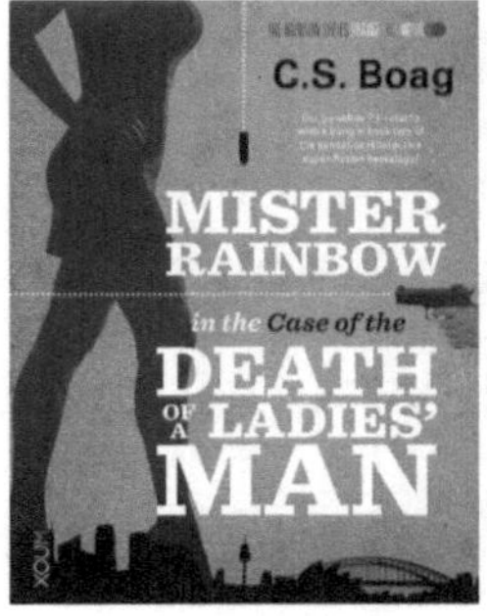

978-1-922057-53-2 (digital)
978-1-922057-54-9 (print)

When Mister Rainbow finds a headless honcho in a Kings Cross alleyway, the tattoo around the corpse's neck leaves little doubt as to its identity. Thomas L. Tycho was everybody's enemy – a trickster, a dirty dealer, and a wide boy who made the mistake of wide boys the world over – not making himself narrower when the gun went off.

The killer's identity, however, proves more elusive – as everybody hated Tommy, anybody could have popped him. His wife, his girl-friend, and half of Sydney's underworld all had motive, but Mister Rainbow smells something fishier than usual, and it's got nothing to do with what's floating in the harbour …

The Case of the Death of a Ladies' Man is the second novel in the sensational Mister Rainbow heptalogy.

Did you enjoy this book?
Why not tell your followers about it?

www.xoum.com.au